F
HAR

THE THIRTY-ONE KINGS

THE THIRTY-ONE KINGS

RICHARD HANNAY RETURNS

ROBERT J. HARRIS

PEGASUS BOOKS
NEW YORK LONDON

To the 78ers – my own personal Die-Hards

His thoughts had been dwelling on his reunion with friends. Those friends would all be scattered. Sandy Clanroyden would be off on some wild adventure. Archie Roylance would be flying, game leg and all. Hannay, Palliser-Yeates, Lamancha, they would all be serving somehow and somewhere.

JOHN BUCHAN, *Sick Heart River*

CONTENTS

PART ONE

THE PILGRIM'S ROAD

1

A MESSAGE FROM ICARUS

——

We were hiking through the familiar landscape of my childhood when the sound of an aeroplane changed everything. That reverberation in the distant air brought back memories very different from my boyhood in the Scottish Lowlands, before my father moved us all to South Africa. It reminded me of a time many years ago when I had fled through these hills as a fugitive from justice, chased by the police and by agents of the Black Stone, who were the real perpetrators of the murder of which I stood accused.

Now, in June of 1940, my circumstances were very different. For one thing my wife Mary was walking at my side, the bright northern sun gleaming on her fair hair, swinging her arms as carelessly as a schoolgirl on the first day of a summer holiday.

For another, I was as far from being a wanted man as it was possible to be. Several times in the past I had been flung into the most extraordinary adventures, such as when the doomed Scudder waylaid me at my front door and pitched me into a deadly cat-and-mouse game with the Black Stone. More than once during the Great War, Sir Walter Bullivant had summoned me from the front lines in France to be sent off on a perilous mission across enemy territory. But now that a fresh conflict had broken out, it appeared that no one required the services of Richard Hannay.

Upon the declaration of war with Germany, I had immediately telegraphed the War Office, asking that my commission might be reinstated so that I could play a full part in the struggle to come. When this appeal met with no reply I wrote directly to Sir Walter Bullivant's successor at the Foreign Office, Lord Charnforth, setting forth my qualifications and experience at greater length than I felt comfortable with, as it goes against the grain to sound my own trumpet.

The dispiriting reply I received was signed by a subordinate I had never heard of and was couched in the most bland and bloodless language. In short it advised me that a large number of requests from former service personnel were currently being processed and that it would require a considerable time to give them all proper consideration, especially in view of more pressing concerns.

My attempts to contact Lord Charnforth directly by phone were rebuffed at every turn by an impenetrable wall of secretaries and minor functionaries who were bent on preventing his lordship from being disturbed by anyone other than the king or the prime minister. I was advised repeatedly to 'bide my time'.

Bide my time! With Europe going up in flames!

What had been loosed upon the world was not, as the poet warned, mere anarchy, but a dreadful iron order that crushed all under the wheels of its relentless advance. Nations to the east and the north had fallen before its lightning aggression and now France, whose mighty army we expected to stand as a bulwark against the coming storm, had crumbled before it. Armour and manpower were flooding through her shattered defences like water through a collapsing dam.

And here was I, as useless as a sword left rusting in the scabbard.

When I could bear inaction no longer, I sought to soothe my frustrations by getting far away from the brass hats in London. Mary insisted on joining me, declaring that I was not to have all the fun while leaving her in the clutches of the local Ladies' Literary Circle. She added that this would be an opportunity to visit friends in Scotland we had not seen in ages.

Tramping through the country where once I had played, fished in the streams, swum in the quiet pools, I hoped to find the calm I so ached for. But today, instead of being comforted, I found my thoughts turning to the very different fate of one of my oldest friends whose recent death haunted me like a melancholy ballad.

Mary's voice broke in on my solemn reverie. 'You're thinking of Ned Leithen again, aren't you?'

Though she was many years younger than I, she had always been the wiser of us two. 'Do you always know what I'm thinking?' I asked in surprise.

'Not always, but when I see that pained crease form between your eyebrows, I can be pretty sure your mind is on thoughts of lost friends. I saw that look many times after the last war whenever you were remembering Peter Pienaar or Launcelot Wake.'

'I had no idea I was so transparent.'

'Only to me, darling. Besides, it was just a few days ago you met with Lamancha, Palliser-Yeates and the others for your private memorial. It's the sort of occasion it takes you a while to shake off.'

Indeed it had been only five days since that gathering in London where we toasted the memory of our late friend Edward Leithen. A noted lawyer and respected MP, Leithen had enjoyed his own share of adventures over the years, but the damage done to his lungs by a gas attack in the Great War had proved to be a slow killer, dogging his footsteps until his doctor gave him no more than a year to live.

Rather than spend the remaining months in comfort, Leithen determined to die on his feet and trekked off into the northern wilderness of Canada in search of a lost soul in need of rescue from more than the viciousness of the Arctic climate. That mission accomplished, Leithen had spent his final days among a brotherhood of missionary priests serving a native tribe devastated by a virulent outbreak of fever.

'It's true,' I admitted. 'I can't help reflecting on the contrast between Ned's final quest and my pleasant walking tour of Dumfries and Galloway.'

'Speaking for myself,' said Mary, 'I'm perfectly happy not to contend with freezing blizzards and mountains of ice. Remember, Dick, he knew his time was up, whatever he did. You're in the best of health with many good years ahead of you.'

'Yes, but what sort of years? Am I going to carry on comfortably tending to the garden, checking the livestock, seeing to repairs around the house? There was a time I did want that, resisted any efforts to drag me away from the good life we've made together. But not now, not while other men are placing their lives at the ultimate hazard.'

'You've done more than your share, you know that,' said Mary. 'But I don't doubt that a call will come.'

'When?' I demanded impatiently. 'Archie Roylance is back in uniform, game leg and all. Lamancha is a member of the War Cabinet with responsibility for munitions. Nobody seems to know where Sandy is, but I've no doubt he's off on some mad jaunt aimed at bloodying Hitler's nose. And me? By the time my call comes I'll be too decrepit to answer it.'

'Don't be ridiculous, Dick,' Mary responded with a chuckle. 'You may have a few grey hairs, but you haven't exactly gone to seed.'

'Oh no? Let me tell you something. Just last week I ran into that dull fellow Welkins.'

'What, the podgy banker?'

'Yes. And do you know what he said to me? He suggested that I take up golf. I ask you, do I look like a man who's so far gone that he's ready to take up golf?'

'No, not yet.' Mary laughed. 'But if you want to stave off that awful day, you can stay in shape by keeping up with me – if you're up to it.'

She tripped off through the heather, so fleet of foot one would have thought the pack on her back weighed nothing at all. I hooked my thumbs through the straps of my own pack and followed as keenly as a man in an old folk tale chasing fairy lights through the gloaming.

For four days we had enjoyed the invigorating freshness of the air sweeping in from the Irish Sea and the unfailing hospitality of the local cottagers. Each morning we were sent off on a hearty breakfast of ham and eggs, while any daytime stops were met with buttered scones and treacle biscuits washed down with mugs of coarse India tea brewed strong enough for a mouse to walk on.

And at night, of course, there was always the obligatory nip of whisky before settling into a rough bed for a welcome sleep.

It had rained heavily in the night but the morning sun had burst through the clouds to cast a bright sheen over the freshly washed landscape. Fed by the overnight rain, the streams bounced and gurgled over pebbles and rocks, as excited as children escaping from school. As the sun slanted towards the west, the cries of plovers and curlews echoed off the hills and the breeze carried a tang of burning peat from the hearth of a far-off cottage.

All at once, as if the musical piping of the birds were the introductory notes of an accompanist, Mary began to sing 'Cherry Ripe', just as she had when I came across her for the first time in the garden at Fosse Manor. It was then that she had identified herself as my contact with instructions from Sir Walter Bullivant. I had been gladly following her orders ever since.

Her song was cut short when we caught the noise of an engine approaching out of the eastern sky. The sound reminded me of how my enemies had once used a plane to pursue me across this very landscape. The memory quickened my pulse and I felt my heels itching to take flight. It was a ridiculous reaction, given that I was no fugitive, but a respected war hero living in comfortable retirement. And yet my instincts told me clearly that something was up.

'Look, he's turning this way,' said Mary, shielding her eyes against the sun to examine the approaching plane.

I could see now that it was a two-man biplane, the two wings fixed together with an arrangement of struts and wires. It wasn't unlike the plane Archie used to take me up in to reconnoitre the German positions before their big push of 1918. The pilot had completed his turn and was now flying directly towards us.

'Yes,' I agreed, 'it's almost as if he were looking for us.'

Mary laughed at my wary tone of voice. 'Dick, I hardly think with all that's happening in France, anyone would spare an aeroplane to seek out a pair of ageing hikers.' She squinted at the approaching craft and pursed her lips. 'It looks like a Tiger Moth. A DH.82, probably, with a de Havilland Gipsy III hundred and twenty horse-power engine.'

I knew she had been considering a position with the Observer Corps, which required the ability to accurately identify aircraft at a distance. To that end she had made an extensive study of aircraft design, both ours and those of the Germans. I also knew she had no intention of taking up such a post so long as I was forced to remain inactive, knowing that it would only exacerbate my own chafing frustration.

While I didn't have her knowledge, my eyes were just as keen. 'I don't see any markings on it,' I noted.

'No, it's a civilian plane,' said Mary, 'but the RAF are drafting them in to use as trainers.'

'Yes, I can see it's a two-man job,' I said. 'But it looks like there's only the pilot aboard. You know, I swear he's waving at us.'

'Probably just being friendly,' said Mary. 'I don't think I could be that casual while flying. I would keep thinking of Icarus flying too close to the sun and his wings melting.'

'Icarus's wings were made from wax and feathers,' I said. 'I'm sure that crate is fashioned out of something more durable.'

Even as I spoke, there came a dull boom, and a gust of smoke blossomed from the rear of the approaching plane. Immediately it began to sway and buck. As it roared directly over us we could see the pilot struggling desperately with the controls.

He plunged so low over the nearest hill that he panicked the sheep grazing there and put them to flight. As the plane disappeared over the hill, we raced up the slope as fast as our legs would carry us with our packs bumping against our backs. We were mounting the crest when we heard the sickening crump of the aircraft striking the ground.

We scrambled down the other side towards the wreck, fragments of loose scree flying up from our heels as we descended. The wheel struts were crushed, the fuselage was cracked in two, and the pilot lay slumped over the controls. As we drew closer I could see sparks sputtering from the electrics and smell the dangerous stink of petroleum in the air.

'Stay back!' I warned Mary.

She ignored my advice and followed me at a run to the plane. When we reached the pilot I undid his safety harness and the two of us hauled him out of the cockpit. Supporting him between us, we hurried to a safe distance. As soon as we laid him out on the ground, there came a stomach-wrenching blast as the fuel tank exploded, setting the ruined craft ablaze.

I snapped loose the strap of his leather flying helmet, pulling it off along with his goggles. The face that stared blearily up at me was youthful, and from its pallor and the blood oozing from his mouth, I could tell he had suffered terrible internal injuries from the impact of the crash.

As Mary yanked open his heavy flying jacket to ease his respiration, he gazed at me with a glint of recognition in his eyes.

'General Hannay!' he croaked.

Somehow my intuition had been correct. He *was* looking for me.

'Rest easy,' I cautioned him. 'We'll find a doctor and get you to a hospital.'

He shook his head and took a feeble grip on my arm. Face contorted in agony, he forced out a hoarse jumble of words: 'London trails . . . latest Dickens . . . missing page . . .'

I felt his fingers slip from my arm, as if he had summoned the last of his strength to deliver this incomprehensible message.

'Please don't strain yourself,' Mary pleaded, gently brushing the sweat-stained hair from his brow.

I could hear in her voice that she was as aware as I that the young man was a goner. However, as a spasm of pain shook his body, he made a further effort at speech. If his words so far had been enigmatic, his final exhortation was utterly baffling.

'Thirty-one kings,' he whispered with his dying breath. 'Find the thirty-one kings!'

2

THE STRANGER ON THE TRAIN

I felt for the pilot's pulse as his eyes fixed sightlessly on the sky from which he had fallen. Turning to Mary, I sadly shook my head. She gazed down pityingly at the young man.

'Dick, what on earth was he talking about? I can't make head nor tail of it.'

'Given the condition he was in, he might just have been raving,' I said dubiously. 'And yet he obviously knew who I was.'

'You were right all along,' she agreed. 'He *was* looking for you. So that must be some sort of message, however garbled.'

I closed the young pilot's eyes and we straightened up. I saw Mary's gaze drift towards the burning wreckage of the crashed Tiger Moth and the plume of acrid smoke that floated above it. Her eyes narrowed and her mouth took on an atypically grim cast. I knew at once that she was thinking of our son Peter John who was now a pilot in the RAF flying sorties across the Channel.

It seemed only fitting that he – who so loved birds of prey that he had raised and trained several of them – should have become one himself. The terrible difference was that the quarry he hunted had talons of its own with which to strike back.

I knew that if Mary did take a post with the Observer Corps she would not simply be scanning the skies for enemy aircraft. She would, whether consciously or not, be keeping watch for the safe return of her son.

With an effort she tore her eyes away from the scene. 'Do you think this was just an accident?'

'It's too much of a coincidence to swallow,' I said. 'I'd bet a pretty penny the plane was sabotaged.'

Before we could speculate further a voice hailed us from a hilltop to the north. A shepherd in a tartan bonnet was shaking his crook at us to get our attention. I waved back and he loped down the hillside towards us with a pair of excited collies scampering after him.

When he reached us he paused to catch his breath and stared down grimly at the pilot. 'When I saw yon plane drappin' oot o' the sky, I kent well there was little hope for the man that flew it. There's enough o' they laddies lost o'er in France wi'oot this.' He removed his bonnet as a mark of respect and stroked his shaggy beard at the tragedy of it. 'It's doonricht lamentable.'

'We're strangers around here,' I told him. 'Can you contact the local authorities to come and take care of him?'

'Aye, Dougal Mackie's place is no far off,' said the shepherd. 'He's had a phone put in, swell that he is. I could fetch the polis on that.'

I indicated to Mary that we should be on our way and we started off at a brisk pace.

'Where are ye off tae?' the shepherd called after us. 'The polis might ask efter ye.'

'We're going to London,' I told him, 'to find some kings.'

✳

By nightfall we managed to reach a small rural station. Flower baskets hung over the platform and a Union Jack fluttered beside the tracks. There were fewer services running because of the wartime demand for coal, so we spent an uncomfortable night in the station waiting room until the morning milk train came chugging along. There were scarcely any passengers, so we easily obtained a carriage to ourselves where we stowed our packs in the overhead rack. The accommodation was luxurious compared to the wooden benches of the waiting room and we looked forward to catching a few extra winks of sleep on the journey to Dumfries.

'I shall have to phone Barbara and let her know we won't be coming after all.' Mary sighed as she gazed out at the wooded glens and gleaming lochs.

'We'll do it another time,' I said. 'Perhaps by then Sandy will be home and we can have a proper reunion.'

'Yes, let's hope so,' said Mary, stifling a yawn. She rested her head against the window and closed her eyes.

I had promised Mary that after our tour of Galloway we would pay a visit to Laverlaw, Sandy Clanroyden's estate in Ettrick, to spend a week there with his wife Barbara and their young daughter Diana. I was less enthusiastic than my wife, not from any lack of enjoyment of Barbara's company or delight in the beauty of the place, but I knew that I would feel Sandy's absence keenly. Knowing he was out somewhere in the world, playing his part in this conflict, made it doubly galling that I was not doing the same.

Sandy and I had served together in France and much further afield. During the Greenmantle affair he had infiltrated the organisation of the beautiful and brilliant German agent Hilda von Einem. She had been grooming a Mohammedan visionary to be the leader of a great uprising that would shift the balance of power in the East in favour of the Kaiser. When her pawn died of cancer, she was so taken in by Sandy's assumed disguise as an Oriental mystic, that she chose him as a replacement. His betrayal of her incensed the woman – but it hurt him too.

When things came to a head, our little band were holding a ruined hill fort at the battle of Erzerum in Turkey. Hilda von Einem approached us under a flag of truce, offering us not only our lives, should we surrender, but renewing her offer to Sandy to stand at her side and become the ruler of a great empire.

The temptation came not from any desire for power on Sandy's part, but from the strange, almost hypnotic attraction she held for him. To say he had fallen in love with her was to put it too mildly, but still he refused, then watched in horror as, while heading back to her own troops, she was killed by a shell from the attacking Russian artillery.

We buried her with honour, but I know her death haunted Sandy for years, right up to the time that he met Barbara during his visit to South America. I had a worrying suspicion that even now he was constantly subjecting himself to the most terrible risks out of a sense of guilt: that he had betrayed that fascinating woman and helplessly watched her die.

As I mused upon the many other scrapes Sandy and I had been through together, the train made a stop and a dozen assorted passengers boarded, some with dogs and one accompanied by a pig. The corridor door to our compartment slid open and in shuffled a tall man dressed in a heavy overcoat. A thick woollen scarf was wrapped around his mouth while the rest of his face was overshadowed by a wide-brimmed fedora.

'Sorry to disturb,' he apologised, his voice muffled by the scarf. 'Got a bit of a chill. Need a quiet spot to shut my eyes. Other compartments full of noise.'

Mary stirred from her slumber and gave him a friendly smile. 'Do sit down,' she invited him. 'We'll do our best not to disturb you.'

'Obliged,' the stranger grunted.

He slumped into the seat opposite us in the spot nearest the door. His eyes closed, his head slouched forward, and his breath sounded slow and steady beneath the covering of his scarf.

We both knew without a word being said to confine our conversation to trivialities. Mary talked some nonsense about fashion while I pretended to be thinking of buying a new bicycle, both of us *sotto voce*.

Our silent companion did not stir, not even when we halted at a tiny station for a minor exchange of passengers. A florid countryman in grubby tweeds and a woman with two squabbling children passed in the corridor but were not inclined to join us, perhaps because the fellow in the coat gave every appearance of ill health.

As we pulled out of the station Mary gave a sigh. 'Do you suppose there's a dining car? I'm feeling rather peckish.'

'I'm sure they'll have coffee available at least,' I assured her.

'In that case I'll go foraging,' she said, standing up and straightening her skirt. 'I'll only be a few minutes.'

The moment she left the compartment the stranger raised his head and his eyes flickered open. He pulled the scarf away from his mouth and tipped back the brim of his hat to reveal a lean face with a large nose and sharp cheekbones. His moustache had turned completely grey, lending a certain affability to his intelligent features.

'It's a relief to be free of that scarf. I was feeling quite stifled.'

I recognised him at once and was not pleased to do so. 'Joseph Bannatyne Barralty.'

He doffed his hat in acknowledgement. 'Sir Richard Hannay. Delighted to meet you again.'

I knew Barralty from a previous encounter some years before. He was what many people would describe as a professional rogue, but in spite of his shady dealings he had never yet fallen into the clutches of the law.

'I'm pleased to see you're not as poorly as you first indicated,' I told him. 'In fact, you look quite well.'

'Speedy recoveries are a speciality of mine. And you, Hannay – a few days in the wilds certainly seem to have put some colour into your cheeks.'

'It's very good of you to say so.'

He removed his hat and set it down on the seat beside him.

'Well, now that the pleasantries are out of the way,' he said, smoothing back his hair, 'we can get down to business.'

'I'm afraid I've no business to offer you,' I said. 'I'm on holiday, in case you didn't know.'

'I'm sure you're familiar with Milton's dictum, "They also serve who only stand and wait". Unless I am much mistaken, your waiting time is over.'

I felt a prickling at the back of my neck, such as often warned me of approaching danger. 'You are much mistaken,' I told him evenly. 'I've been a civilian for many years now and intend to continue in that avenue. I would advise you to do the same or one day you will be tripped up by your own supposed cleverness.'

He tutted and shook his head. 'Would that things were as you say, but in a time of crisis such as we are living through now, there will be precious little peace for either one of us. There are too many pressures, too many opportunities, and in your case the call of duty.'

Barralty spoke pleasantly but I was not deceived.

'You know, I really preferred your company when you were still asleep,' I said pointedly. 'You're proving to be rather tiresome.'

He leaned forward and fixed his shrewd eyes upon me. 'There is no reason for any antagonism between us. You will recall, Mr Hannay, that although we were on opposite sides during that Halverson affair, we nevertheless parted on reasonable terms.'

My hackles rose. 'If you've turned Nazi, Barralty, I don't think we'll be parting quite so amicably this time.'

'I'm no Nazi,' Barralty scoffed. 'You surely can't think that.'

'No,' I conceded, 'but I do know you always have an eye for the main chance, and I suppose their money is as good as anybody's, provided there's enough of it to quiet your conscience.'

Barralty looked pained. 'I assure you, Hannay, that my . . . associates in this matter are patriots of the highest standing.'

'Patriots who don't mind killing their own,' I reminded him with some bitterness.

'That chap in the plane?' Barralty cocked a dismissive eyebrow. 'As soon as he realised something was up with the engine, he should have put down or bailed out. Instead he pressed on with his search for you, even to his own destruction. Which suggests to me that he had a message of some import to pass on.'

'It would have been better if you asked him about that yourself. Unfortunately that's no longer an option.'

Barralty spoke in a measured voice, but there was a threat underlying it. 'I'd be very much obliged if you would share that message with me.'

'If you're looking for a letter,' I said, spreading my hands, 'I swear I haven't got one.'

'It wouldn't be written down,' he countered. 'I'm sure it was passed on by word of mouth.'

'You're out of luck there,' I told him coolly. 'He didn't survive the crash. And dead men have very little to say for themselves.'

'If you received no word, no call to arms, then what possessed you to abandon your pleasant holiday and head south in such haste?'

'I'm tired of eating burnt ham and greasy eggs for breakfast,' I said. 'I got a sudden yearning for kippers and French toast.'

The side of his mouth twisted unpleasantly. 'I'm afraid flippancy really won't serve, Hannay. You know I have the deepest respect for you, but I am in the employ of men who expect results, not witticisms.'

As he said this, his right hand slipped into the pocket of his coat. I had no doubt as to what was concealed there.

'Would you really go so far?' I queried.

Barralty's eyes narrowed. 'Mr Hannay, it is not to my taste to have your lovely wife return to a scene of violence, but you really mustn't press me. Now tell me what message that unfortunate man brought you.'

I saw the muscles tense in his neck and knew his finger was tight against the trigger.

'I wish I could oblige you, old man,' I responded with mock affability, 'but I really have no idea what you're talking about.'

'In that case I will have to insist that both you and Mrs Hannay get off at the next stop with me. Some friends of mine are waiting there with a car to take us to an isolated location where you can enjoy a period of quiet seclusion.'

'I'm sure the peace and quiet would be restful, but I couldn't put you to all that trouble. Besides, my wife has her heart set on lunch at Claridge's tomorrow.'

'I am doing my best to be civilised,' said Barralty through gritted teeth, 'but you are making it impossible. My instructions are clear. You are to leave the train with me, or you will not leave it at all. Neither one of you.'

It was at that moment that the corridor door slid open and Mary entered.

3

THE IMAGINARY EX

Sliding the door shut behind her, she flashed a casual smile at Barralty. 'Oh, I see you're awake,' she observed pleasantly. 'So glad you're feeling better, Mr . . . I'm sorry, I didn't catch your name.'

There was a large cup of tea in her hand which she struggled to keep from splashing as the train jolted suddenly.

Barralty's face took on a ruthless cast. 'Please be seated, Mrs Hannay,' he ordered in a stern voice.

Ignoring him completely, Mary addressed me in her sweetest tones. 'Dick, darling, I'm sure you're parched, so I brought you some tea. It's good and hot, just the way you like it.'

Barralty's hard stare warned me not to move as he began to slide the gun out of his pocket. 'Please sit down!' he snapped.

Mary glanced down at the tea. 'Oh, I'm awfully sorry, darling,' she said with a pout. 'I completely forgot to add milk.'

With a swift twist of her wrist she flung the scalding contents of the cup directly into Barralty's face.

He leapt up with a howl of pain, sweeping his left sleeve across his stinging eyes. As he tore the pistol free of his pocket, I lunged forward and grabbed him by the arms, pinning them to his side. We lurched about the compartment in a clumsy waltz, bashing against the seats in the confined space.

I lowered my head and butted him in the face. His finger tightened reflexively on the trigger, firing a shot through the floor. With a curse he shook off my blow and twisted violently this way and that, trying to break loose and bring his revolver to bear. I knew if my grip slackened for an instant he would be able to put a bullet in me.

I felt Mary squeeze past my back. A sudden breeze blew through the compartment as she flung the outer door wide open.

'Thanks for that, darling,' I panted. 'I'm sure Mr Barralty will appreciate some fresh air.'

With that I threw all my weight into a desperate shove that sent him stumbling backwards and out into empty space. As I heaved the door shut, I saw him tumble down an embankment. Mary peered through the glass just as he disappeared from view.

'Do you suppose he's all right?' she wondered. 'I wasn't looking to break his neck.'

'I shouldn't worry about him,' I said. 'He specialises in speedy recoveries.' I drew a deep breath and eyed my wife with admiration. 'I must say, it was very resourceful of you to fetch a weapon from the catering car.'

'There was obviously something queer about him,' she explained, 'and I thought if I left the two of you alone for a few minutes he might tip his hand.'

'He certainly did that.'

She set aside the empty cup and sat down. I joined her and gave her the gist of what had passed between us.

'Do you think if it came to it, he would really have shot you?' Mary pondered with a frown.

'I'd like to think not. But if we meet again, I won't give him the benefit of the doubt.'

We both looked up as the corridor door opened. There stood the conductor, a portly man with luxuriant whiskers, throwing curious glances about the compartment.

'Ye'll excuse me for disturbing you, I'm sure,' he said, 'but a passenger in the next compartment reported hearing a gunshot.'

'A shot?' said Mary. She could not have looked more innocent if she had been a newborn babe. 'How extraordinary.'

'Oh, I know what happened,' I said. 'The outer door there came open. Must be a faulty catch. I had to slam it shut pretty sharply – you know, for safety's sake.'

'Yes, it made quite a crack,' said Mary.

'Ah, that will be it, I'm sure,' said the conductor. He pulled out a pocket watch and checked it as we slowed down. 'Killywhan, spot on time,' he declared proudly as we pulled into the station.

Slipping past him, I glanced out at the platform. Barralty had said there would be friends waiting for him here.

'Is something amiss, sir?' the conductor enquired.

Even as he spoke I saw an agitated fellow in a trenchcoat prowling up and down the platform. Everyone else there looked like an ordinary traveller awaiting the train. I was trying to think of a story to tell the conductor when Mary piped up.

'Yes, there is actually. It's my ex-husband. I'm afraid he may be out there looking for us.'

'What, here at Killywhan?' the conductor exclaimed, as if such scandalous doings were unheard of in this particular village.

I pressed my back to the carriage wall, out of sight of the window. 'That's him out there in the trenchcoat.'

Mary put a hand to her mouth to stifle a horrified gasp. 'Would you believe he actually had a detective follow us onto the train?' she said in anguished tones. 'Luckily we managed to shake him off.'

'The possessive type, is he?' said the conductor with a sorrowful shake of his head. 'These modern divorces gie rise to muckle complications.'

'He's an absolute beast,' said Mary with feeling. 'He's from Wolverhampton.'

'Aye, well, that would explain it,' said the conductor sagely.

'If he gets on the train we'll never get loose of him,' I said. 'I say, could you do us an enormous favour?'

The conductor glanced at Mary whose plaintive expression would have melted the heart of a hangman.

'I suppose I could,' he agreed as the train came to a halt, 'for the sake of heading off trouble.'

'Please tell him that his friend Mr Barralty was forced to get off at the previous stop and that he must join him there as quickly as possible.'

'The previous stop, as quickly as possible,' the conductor repeated, nodding. He gave a chuckle. 'It's quite the lark, isn't it? Wait till I tell the wife about this.'

Mary handed him Barralty's fedora. 'Oh, and could he return the gentleman's hat to him. He left it behind in his hurry.'

While passengers disembarked and fresh travellers boarded, the man in the trenchcoat moved rapidly along the platform, scrutinising the windows in search of Barralty. The conductor climbed down and hailed him before he reached our carriage.

I could not overhear what was said for the hissing of the engine and the blare of the Tannoy, but the message had the desired effect. The man bolted for the exit, presumably to join another member of the gang who was waiting outside with the car. The conductor gave us a thumbs-up sign and climbed back aboard.

As the train pulled out I sat down beside Mary again. 'You never told me you had another husband,' I joked.

'A little mystery is good for any marriage,' she answered demurely.

At Dumfries we caught the first southbound train and I whiled away the journey trying to make sense of the pilot's garbled message. I wrote his last words down in the hope that their meaning would be clearer when I could read them over.

London trails, latest Dickens, missing page,
and, most puzzling of all,
Find the thirty-one kings.

After a couple of changes of train we arrived at St Pancras in the late afternoon. We took a cab to the house in Great Charles Street that Mary had inherited from her Wymondham aunts. Here we took time for a quick bath and a change of clothes. Mary then telephoned our people at Fosse Manor to let them know we were back from Scotland while I headed off into town.

I had a hearty dislike for London in wartime. There were too many uniforms in the street, barrage balloons jostled in the sky, and the rooftops were crowned with anti-aircraft guns. Out on the front line you were face to face with the enemy and had your chance to confront him directly. Here the danger was unseen and all was tension and nervous expectation.

As I walked towards my destination, a lorry rumbled past filled with young soldiers singing a ribald song I recognised from my own army days. I wondered where they were headed and hoped that the goal I had in mind for myself was the correct one and not a wild goose chase.

On the journey south, as I pondered the cryptic words of the dying pilot, I became increasingly certain that his reference to 'trails' was in fact the name of a bookshop: Traill's in Mayfair. I was well acquainted with the owner of the place, though his identity was unknown to almost everyone else. An eccentric bibliophile was the general opinion, and not entirely untrue, but still wide of the mark in many respects. He was, in fact, one of the most remarkable men I have ever encountered.

I stopped outside the shop and looked up at the sign which was painted in faded red and green: *Traill's Book Shop, Dealers in both New and Antique Volumes.* Casting an eye over the window, I spotted a pair of new mysteries by Agatha Christie as well as Household's recent shocker, which I confess I rather enjoyed. What I did not see, of course, was a brand new novel by Dickens. Not even a new edition of one of his classics.

A bell jingled above me as I entered, but the few customers inside were too absorbed in examining the bookshelves to pay any attention to me. I hesitantly approached the counter where the assistant, a tall individual with slicked-back hair, regarded me superciliously through his pince-nez.

'Can I help you, sir?'

He looked so utterly respectable that I felt quite foolish saying to him, 'Yes, I'm looking for the latest novel by Dickens.'

He raised a sardonic eyebrow. 'Do you mean Charles Dickens, the long-deceased novelist?'

'Yes,' I persisted. 'I believe he has a brand new book out.'

'Indeed, sir. Let me see if I can help you.'

For a moment I thought by helping me he meant call for an ambulance to carry me off to a lunatic asylum. However, instead of reaching for the phone, he turned to the bookshelf behind him. He considered carefully for a few moments before taking down a slim, leather-bound volume which he handed to me.

'Perhaps this is what you're looking for,' he said in a tone that was a mixture of condescension and pity.

There was no writing on the cover so I opened the book and, in some confusion, flipped through the pages. They were all blank.

I looked up at the assistant and saw that he was regarding me expectantly. I felt as though I had stepped into a scene from *Alice's Adventures in Wonderland* and that the individual standing before me was some demented cousin of the Mad Hatter.

I had no idea how to react, then I recalled the pilot's words.

'There's a page missing,' I said tentatively.

He gave a curious frown and reached for the book which I gladly surrendered to him.

'If you have a complaint to make,' he informed me stiffly, 'you will have to speak to the proprietor. I believe you know the way.'

He inclined his head towards the stairway at the back of the shop, then reached a hand under the counter. I was quite sure he was pressing a button that would alert the man waiting upstairs to my imminent arrival.

Confident now that I was on the right track, I climbed the steps to the upper floor. Here the walls were crammed with volumes on every abstruse subject under the sun and the tables were laid out with vintage maps and engravings. I glanced around to ensure that I was completely alone, then approached one wall which I knew concealed a secret behind its display of false book spines.

Pressing the bogus copy of Walton's *The Compleat Angler*, I felt a catch release and with a slight shove I opened the hidden door. As I entered the room beyond, the door swung back into place behind me. There, behind a desk covered in papers and playing cards, sat the large, unmistakable figure of John Scantlebury Blenkiron. In his hand was a pistol which was pointed directly at me.

4

THE ECCENTRIC BIBLIOPHILE

I fixed a disgruntled gaze on the pistol. 'You know, I'm delighted to see you, Blenkiron,' I told him, 'but if people keep drawing guns on me I'm liable to get testy.'

Heaving himself to his feet, Blenkiron set the gun aside with an embarrassed grin. He manoeuvred his considerable bulk around the desk and strode towards me with an outstretched hand.

'Dick, you old war horse!' he greeted me in his pleasant American drawl.

We shook hands heartily and he slapped me on the shoulder.

'Sorry about the reception.' Blenkiron rolled his eyes in self-deprecation. 'These days I reckon I'm as jumpy as a barefoot man on a rattlesnake farm. Why, if old Grandma Blenkiron herself walked in here, I'd have to frisk her before I let her sit down.'

'And I suppose that's the reason for all this nonsense about Dickens concocting a new bestseller from beyond the grave.'

'I know all these code words are kind of foolish,' he admitted, 'but only a lunatic would walk into a bookstore expecting to find a brand new novel by Charles Dickens – a lunatic or somebody who'd got my message.'

'So did you have your gun ready in case some crazed madman stumbled upon your secret room?' I queried.

Blenkiron's brow darkened as he answered, 'No, I was armed in case it wasn't you but somebody else who'd intercepted the message and figured it out just the way you did.'

'Intercept it? How would they do that?'

'They couldn't unless they were on the inside,' said Blenkiron, 'and that's the most vexing part of the whole business. Look, let's have a drink. I know I could stand one.'

While he busied himself at the drinks cabinet, I surveyed his hidden lair. On one wall was a map of France and the Low Countries scrawled with a jumble of multi-coloured arrows that illustrated just how rapidly the situation there was evolving. The bookshelves were crammed with volumes on code breaking, military strategy and politics. On the desk a heap of files and telegrams surrounded a deck of cards laid out in a half finished game of Patience. It was somehow comforting to know that simple card games were still his favoured way of relaxing his busy mind.

Like me, Blenkiron had a background as a mining engineer and we had been comrades in arms at Erzerum and in France in 1918 when he commanded a rag-tag unit that helped me to hold the line against the German attack. Logistics and intelligence gathering, however, had always been his strongest suits. In the years since the war he had confined his activities to business and politics so that his large frame had taken on the proportions of a man used to a more sedentary life.

Once he had supplied each of us with a glass of Glenfiddich, we sat down in a pair of leather armchairs with a small round table between us. He set his glass down while he lit one of his thin black cigars.

'Well, Dick,' he said, taking a long puff, 'when you make yourself scarce, you don't kid around. Why didn't you hole up in a nice, cosy hotel where I could reach you by phone or telegram?'

'The point was to be out of touch,' I said. 'To be honest, I was in a bit of a funk from having so many doors slammed in my face.'

'That man of yours at Fosse Manor, Godstow, is a tight-lipped son of a sea cook,' said Blenkiron, 'but he finally spilled where you'd taken off to. Given that you were hiking through the wilds, sending young Tommy Llewellyn up there in a plane seemed the best bet for tracking you down.'

'You heard about the crash, I suppose.'

He gave a grim nod. 'I'd bet a gold mine it was no accident.'

'You'd win that bet,' I confirmed, and proceeded to tell him about my run-in with Barralty.

Blenkiron got up and made a tour of the room while I spoke. He brought the bottle back with him and refreshed our glasses as he sat down.

'I don't have to tell you,' he said, 'that right now things are sitting on the edge of a very sharp razor. The newspapers are keeping up a confident front, as if any day now the French are going to make another stand, like they did on the Marne. But the truth is, we're way past that point. The game's up and all we can do is grab our chips and run.'

There was such gloom in his voice that I took a large swallow of Scotch and slumped back in my chair. 'How on earth did it come to this?' I wondered aloud. 'I mean, the French soldier is as brave as any and their generals have been preparing for years for a day like this.'

Blenkiron leaned forward and ran a finger around the rim of his glass. 'Ever been to a bullfight, Dick?'

'I can't say that I have,' I said, lighting my pipe and taking a tentative puff.

'Well, forget all that baloney about courage and skill,' said Blenkiron. 'It's trickery, pure and simple. You see, the matador makes a big show of waving a cape about on his left arm. Now the sight of that red rag gets the bull all riled up and he charges the cape, getting his horns tangled up in a big heap of empty air. The matador meanwhile has his sword in his other hand and stabs at the bull from his blind side. See how it works?'

'Yes, but I don't see what that has to do with the Germans.'

With a jerk of his thumb Blenkiron directed my gaze towards the map on the wall. 'Well, that advance they made in northern Belgium, that was the red rag, and our bull went after it with troops, tanks and aircraft. Then Hitler sent his sword through our south side, through the Ardennes.'

'The Ardennes? That's a hard country for tanks.'

'It's a hard country for anybody, which made it twice as big a surprise. Even when the Germans poured through in force, most of our generals still thought that was the feint, not all the ruckus up north. Instead of cutting your guys off from the Dutch ports, their plan was to sweep along to the south, then turn north, and wrap up the whole caboodle in one tight noose.'

When I studied the map more closely, the details confirmed Blenkiron's analysis.

'It can't be that bad,' I protested. 'Surely the French will make a stand somewhere.'

Blenkiron grimaced. 'This isn't nineteen fourteen. There'll be no trenches this time because things are moving too damned fast. Sure, some of their boys have shown they have guts, but they're scattered and demoralised now. They're in no shape to organise a counter-attack.'

I felt myself stiffen. 'Are you telling me they're going to surrender?'

'They'll call it an armistice,' said Blenkiron with a shrug, 'but it's as like a surrender as a pig resembles a hog. The battle for France is all over, Dick. You Brits are on your own now and the only ally you've got left is that stretch of water that separates Dover from Calais.'

I managed to summon a grin. 'Oh, I wouldn't say that. We have you, don't we?'

Blenkiron chortled. 'Yeah, whenever you're in a bind you can always count on John S. to lend a hand.' He raised his whisky glass in a kind of toast.

'The fact is,' he continued, 'President Roosevelt saw the direction things were taking a couple of years ago and asked me personally to come over and renew some of my old acquaintances on this side of the ocean. So I had this place tidied up' – he waved a hand about the room – 'and started to build up a network of contacts, while selling a few books along the way.'

'Well, you won't sell many as long as that specimen downstairs is manning the counter,' I said.

'Old Henry puts on a good front for the customers,'

said Blenkiron. 'It doesn't pay to be too welcoming when the real business is being carried out behind the scenes. To look at him you'd never suppose he's an expert in unarmed combat. And in case that isn't enough, under the counter he has a Browning automatic hidden inside a hollowed-out copy of *Vanity Fair*.'

'I have to say, you've taken your time bringing me into this network of yours,' I said, trying my best not to sound peevish.

Blenkiron favoured me with a wry smile. 'As you well know, Dick, I'm accustomed to playing a lone hand – but I choose my cards carefully and keep them close to my chest. All along you've been the ace up my sleeve, and I wanted to keep you well out of the picture in the hope that people on both sides might forget all about Richard Hannay.'

'It certainly felt to me like you succeeded,' I noted drily. 'So why now? What's so vital that it was worth sending that boy at the risk of his life to summon me here? And who on earth are the thirty-one kings?'

Leaning back, Blenkiron took a pull on his cigar and blew a circle of smoke towards the ceiling. 'That's the nub of it. We don't know, and we only have a few days to find out.'

'You're not making things any clearer.'

'Just let me tell you the story.' Blenkiron tapped some ash from the end of his cigar as he gathered his thoughts. 'A few weeks ago I started receiving coded messages from a fellow going under the name of Mr Roland. He included the names of one or two trustworthy individuals who would vouch for him without revealing his identity.

A week ago he said he had vital information to bring to London about these thirty-one kings – said the whole future of the war could hang on it.'

'Have you any clue as to what he was referring?'

Blenkiron got up and fetched a Bible from his desk. 'All I could come up with – and that's only because I'm a solid Presbyterian born and raised – is here in the King James.' He sat down and began flipping through the pages. 'Book of Joshua, chapter twelve, verses nine to twenty-four. These verses list the thirty-one kings defeated by Joshua when he conquered the promised land.'

He passed me the open Bible and I glanced down the list. It began with 'The king of Jericho, one; the king of Ai, which is beside Bethel, one;' and ended with the words, 'All the kings, thirty and one'.

'I've read that list over and over until I can recite the whole gang of them by heart, but I still can't winkle any sort of message out of it,' said Blenkiron.

'Perhaps the whole thing is bogus,' I suggested, laying the book down.

'It's not flummery,' said Blenkiron. 'Not by a long shot. The Germans got wind of this too and it set Berlin buzzing like a hornets' nest. They're just as keen to get their hands on Mr Roland's little secret as I am.'

'So where is your Mr Roland now?'

'Well, I know he made his way to Paris and we were supposed to arrange a rendezvous there. But since then silence. He seems to have disappeared off the face of the earth.'

'What do you suppose happened?'

Blenkiron's normally placid features darkened.

'Most likely he's fallen into enemy hands. For some time the Germans have had an agent in Paris they refer to as Klingsor. I'm pretty sure he's put the bag on Roland and is holding him there.'

'You don't suppose they've killed him or spirited him off to Berlin?'

Blenkiron shook his head and lit a fresh cigar. 'If this information of his is so darned important they'll keep him alive and try to get it out of him. And they don't have to risk smuggling him out of Paris because in a few days' time their own army will be goose-stepping down the Champs-Élysées.'

I stared at him, aghast. 'Do you mean the Germans are going to walk in without any resistance?'

'That's right. What passes for the French government are on the run somewhere around Bordeaux, and to save Paris from being obliterated they've declared it an open city. That means there will be no French troops there to defend it.'

'It sickens me to think of Hitler getting his filthy hands on Paris,' I said, 'but I suppose it's that or see the whole city bombed into ruins.'

'So wherever Klingsor is holding Mr Roland, he only has to sit tight and the Reich will come to him,' Blenkiron continued. 'What we have to do is find Roland, bust him out and get him back to London pronto. And because of this open-city policy it can't be a military operation.' He eyed me squarely. 'I need you to go in as a civilian.'

Of all the roles I had envisioned for myself, this certainly wasn't one of them. 'I want to do my bit – you can have no doubts about that – but it's been years since I got myself into this sort of a caper.'

'Dick, this is such a damnably important business there's only one man fit for it,' Blenkiron said gravely, 'and that's the man I trust most in the whole world. Nobody else has your knack for pulling off this kind of a job.'

'I don't know that I'd call it a knack. It's mostly sheer stubbornness and luck.'

'Whatever's at the bottom of it, somehow you always hit the target square in the bull's-eye,' Blenkiron asserted roundly. 'Mind you, I'm not going to minimise the opposition, because they're a pretty desperate bunch and there's not much they'll stick at.'

'I take it you mean this man Klingsor and, of course, the full might of the Wehrmacht.'

'Them too,' Blenkiron agreed, 'but right now I'm talking about the opposition smack dab on our own doorstep. By your own account you've already had a run-in with them and I can promise you they haven't quit yet.'

'You talk like the whole country is riddled with Nazi agents.'

'If it was just a case of some Nazi spies, I could have them rounded up pretty sharply and tipped into a nice deep dungeon. But no, these characters aren't Nazis, or even traitors, strictly speaking. They just want to scupper anything that might get in the way of a peace deal with Hitler.'

'A peace deal with Hitler?' I recoiled in spite of myself. 'They can't be serious!'

'The way they see it, if we carry on with a war against Germany, we're in for a hard beating.' Blenkiron made no effort to conceal his distaste. 'It's the worst kind of fatalism, the kind that makes you give up before you've even taken the chance.'

'But how many of them can there be?'

'More than you might think, and they're in every walk of life, including inside your Parliament. And they all think of themselves as patriots.'

'It's a queer sort of patriotism to act against the interests of your own country.'

'Well, Dick, there are interests and there are goddamned interests. What drives these people is a sort of pessimism. You see, you and I will fight on to the last bullet and then go down flinging rocks. But these Johnnies have a different view. When victory seems impossible, they want to settle for the sort of defeat that will go least hard on them.'

'You mean surrender,' I said bleakly.

'A surrender on terms, if you will. They see Hitler steamrollering his way across Europe and they reckon nothing can stand up to him. For them France's fall is a certainty, and damn me if they're not right about that. They argue that as a matter of sheer practicality we need to swallow our pride and cut a deal with the Führer while we still can.'

'They're fools if they think he can be trusted.'

'Sure enough. By my reckoning, when you sup with this particular devil, you'd best have a spoon as long as the Trans-Pacific. Still, the deal he's offering is mighty tempting to certain parties: leave Europe to him and Britain can have her empire and anything else that's up for grabs.'

'It will never happen,' I scoffed. 'Churchill would never agree to it.'

'No, he wouldn't,' Blenkiron agreed. 'That's why these men are planning to get rid of him.'

5

ENCOUNTER WITH A
WING THREE-QUARTER

―――

'You're not talking assassination, surely?' I exclaimed.

'No, no,' said Blenkiron, waving his cigar dismissively. 'Even if they had the sand for it, they know that would just rile folks up against Hitler even more. What they figure is, if things keep on the way they're going, with country after country falling to the Germans, the British people will lose the gumption for a fight. That will give them the chance they need to oust Churchill and replace him with somebody a sight more amenable. Take it from me, there's no shortage of candidates.'

'If your lot were to mix in with us,' I pointed out, 'that would scupper their plans for sure.'

'Look, FDR will give Churchill all the help he can in the form of supplies and intelligence,' Blenkiron explained, 'but as for bringing the USA into the war, that's going to take a bit of time. That's why Britain has to hold out.'

'The mood right now is definitely to fight on,' I asserted.

'But that can change. My job here is to give you Brits an edge and keep you in the game. Our peace-loving friends know that, and now that I've made my move, they're pulling out all the stops to stymie me.'

'And you think it all hinges on Mr Roland and his thirty-one kings?'

Blenkiron nodded emphatically. 'If the information he promised is as big a deal as he claims, it could swing the top dogs in this country firmly into line behind Churchill, and we know that old Winston will resist Hitler to the last drop of blood.'

I glanced at the map which showed the German thrust driving unstoppably westward. 'How much time do we have before they take Paris?'

'Three or four days at the most,' Blenkiron answered grimly. 'That's why you have to go now. It's as dangerous as all get out, I know, but sometimes you have to grab the poker by the hot end.'

I tapped the stem of my pipe against my palm. 'I'd be a lot happier if I were making this trip with at least one of the old team at my side.'

'I'm itching to come with you,' said Blenkiron, ruefully patting his paunch, 'but as you can see, too many years of easy living have taken their toll. I was never a genuine soldier like you, and right now I'd only slow you down.'

'Can we get hold of Sandy Clanroyden?' I asked him.

A cloud passed across Blenkiron's cherubic face and he took a sip of whisky as he considered his words.

'Lord Clanroyden has been on the continent for some considerable time. He's in deep, far too deep for us to bring him out, even for a job as big as this.'

The news didn't surprise me. Over the years Sandy had adopted new identities in every corner of the world, false names he could slip into like an old suit of clothes whenever the need arose. He seemed to have a knack for establishing himself in a spot even before anyone else suspected trouble was liable to break out there.

I nodded slowly. 'I suspected as much when I heard nothing of him. You'd think for Barbara's sake he'd stop risking his fool neck.'

'Like you, you mean,' said Blenkiron with a dry chuckle.

'It's a different sort of foolishness in my case. No matter how far I travel and what dangers I face, I know where my true home is and I'll always be drawn back there. But with Sandy the attraction has always been the other way, always venturing out there in search of some fate no one else can guess at.'

'It's true that it's darn close to a fever with that gent,' Blenkiron agreed, 'but that sickness of his has served us well too often to force a cure on him.'

'So I'm on my own this time.'

'Not quite, Dick. I've recruited a few friendly desperados who'll hook up with you once you're in France.' Blenkiron grinned. 'I call them my Special Reserve.'

'Special Reserve?' I echoed. 'It sounds like a fine whisky.'

Blenkiron's grin broadened. 'These gentlemen have been matured like a good malt and now they're ready to step up. Speaking of fine whisky,' he said, reaching again for the bottle, 'let's have a last toast before I send you on your way.'

Blenkiron provided me with some additional pieces of information that would prove valuable once I reached Paris, as well as his assurance that I would soon be contacted by another of his agents. On my way out I passed Henry wrapping a volume of poetry for a customer with the same supercilious air he had used on me.

As soon as I stepped outside, the rumble of traffic and the gritty smell of the city hit me with the impression that I had moved from the secret world of intrigue and concealed rooms back into everyday life with its commonplace routine. I was just looking round for a cab when one pulled up right in front of me.

'Hop in, guv'nor!' the driver invited me cheerily. 'I'll get you where you're going quick as a lick.'

I opened the back door, but before I could get in the noise of a powerful engine made me turn. I saw a motorcycle, the rider hunched over the handlebars, roaring down the pavement directly towards me.

At the last instant the motorcyclist slammed on the brakes and swerved to a halt mere inches from my foot. He lashed out with his left leg and kicked the taxi door shut with the sole of his boot. Ignoring the violent cursing of the cabbie, he turned to me and pushed up his goggles. 'General Hannay, sir, I'd be obliged if you would climb up here behind me.'

Taken aback by his abrupt arrival, my first thought was to get rid of the man. 'I already have a cab, thank you,' I responded brusquely.

From the corner of his eye he kept tabs on the taxi driver who was shaking his fist in a crimson fury. 'Sir,' he persisted, 'I am a close friend of Mr Dickens. I take it you enjoyed his new novel.'

That got my attention.

'It was a real page turner,' I said, meeting the steady gaze of his clear grey eyes.

'Sir, if we could go,' he pressed urgently.

I couldn't say whether it was his use of Blenkiron's password or his Scottish accent that inclined me to trust him but I felt confident I was placing myself in a safe pair of hands. I had no sooner climbed up behind him and wrapped my arms around his waist than he gunned the engine and we roared off.

From behind us came a violent screech of tyres. Glancing back, I saw the cabbie execute a tight turn and come racing after us.

'He must be desperate for business,' I remarked above the growl of the bike engine.

'He is desperate, and that's for certain,' the motorcyclist agreed. 'Please hold on tightly.'

He bore down on the throttle and the bike shot forward like a racehorse, weaving deftly through the traffic. The cabbie accelerated to top speed and ignored every rule of the road in order to keep us in sight. The air was filled with the angry horns of other drivers whose path the pursuing taxi cut across.

My eyes blurred and my stomach lurched as our bike shot the narrow gap between two red London buses. My new acquaintance wrenched us into an alleyway, glancing off two dustbins and knocking an empty cardboard box high into the air. We made a sharp corner into another tight alleyway, sending a cat screeching for safety. A tramp rummaging through the refuse at the rear of a restaurant almost climbed straight up the wall in his haste to escape as we whooshed past.

We emerged into an open street, leaving the taxi far behind. The motorcyclist twisted his way rapidly through the cars and buses and pulled up at the edge of Hyde Park. From Speaker's Corner I could hear the stentorian tones of a resolute pacifist declaiming that Britain must withdraw completely from the European conflict for the sake of peace, humanity and several other virtuous things.

I dismounted with a sense of relief that we had survived our hare-brained ride. A few passers-by gawked at us as if we had materialised out of thin air, and I was grateful that no policemen had witnessed our breaking of so many traffic laws.

'It's generally unwise to get on the bad side of a London cabbie,' I informed the motorcyclist as he climbed off his bike and kicked out the stand to keep it upright.

He removed his goggles and helmet and gave a faint smile. 'I don't think you and he had the same destination in mind.' He briefly surveyed the traffic to confirm that we had indeed shaken off our pursuer.

'And what makes you think that?' I asked.

'Oh, the fact that he was waiting up the road with his engine idling and only moved when he saw you coming out of Traill's.'

My new acquaintance looked to be in his late twenties and, though he was of middle height and slightly built, it was obvious he had a considerable wiry strength. There was a calm watchfulness about him that impressed me as his sharp grey eyes took in every aspect of our surroundings, assessing safety here, a shadow of danger there.

'Mr Blenkiron's man Henry called me to say you were here and that I should hurry over and keep an eye on you. I must say I'm very glad to make your acquaintance, General Hannay.'

'It's my view that a man should not be addressed as "general" unless he is wearing the uniform,' I told him.

'Sir Richard it is then,' he corrected himself.

'That will do until we're better acquainted, Mr . . . ?'

'Galt, sir, John Galt.'

Something about that name struck me as familiar and I quickly reappraised the fellow. I had seen that slim pale face in a photograph some years ago.

'Galt, eh? Tell me, Mr Galt, have you ever been one for the game of rugby?'

A nostalgic smile lit his finely drawn features. 'I admit I was a furious beast at it in my younger days. I played for Cambridge.'

'And for Scotland, I recall. You were wing three-quarter in that famous victory over Australia. All the papers were full of your praises.'

'It was a devil of a scrap,' he said, 'and we were lucky to pull it off as we did.'

'Lucky, perhaps, but some bold play on your part, I recall, clinched the match in the dying seconds, Mr Galt.'

'I did my bit,' he admitted modestly. 'And people generally call me Jaikie.'

'It's a pleasure to know you, Jaikie,' I said offering him my hand. 'We're in a tougher game now, I think.'

'But still on the same team,' said he as we shook.

'That's quite a steed you've got there,' I said, eyeing the bike.

'She's a proper beauty, isn't she?' he agreed proudly. 'She's a modified five hundred cc Empire Star and at a push she can top a hundred m.p.h.'

'After the ride we just had, I can quite believe it.'

'If you'd care to get back aboard, sir, I can take you wherever it is you want to go. I promise to take it easy this time.'

As we climbed onto the bike I said, 'Perhaps one day you can tell me the whole story of that legendary match.'

'Oh, we'll have plenty of time for that,' he assured me. 'I'm going with you to Paris.'

6

SHELL GAME

___

When we reached the house in Great Charles Street, I showed Jaikie where to park his bike in the back garden.

'You don't suppose any malevolent taxi drivers are likely to come looking for us here, do you?' I asked.

'Mr Blenkiron has a couple of men keeping watch from across the street,' Jaikie assured me. 'They'll shoo off any unwelcome visitors.'

'Mr Blenkiron's obviously been very busy during my enforced retirement.'

'He excels at those sort of arrangements, sir, as you well know.'

Once inside we found the place had been thoroughly aired out and the housekeeper, Mrs Broyles, was conjuring up an evening meal out of some hurriedly gathered ingredients.

Mary appeared in a floral patterned dress, jotting a few reminders in her notebook.

'I've spoken to our people at Fosse and they seem pleased that we're back from Scotland,' she said. 'They want to know when we'll be home.'

'You as soon as you like. I'm likely to be gone a little while yet.'

'Yes, I was rather expecting that,' said my wife.

I introduced my new friend and told Mary that he and I would be leaving for France first thing. 'Once there, we're going to be taking a few risks,' I added.

Mary sighed. 'Are you sure I can't come along? France is so lovely at this time of year – under normal circumstances.'

'I'm sure you'll find plenty to keep you busy here. In fact I'll be surprised if you aren't in uniform by the time I get back.'

'You won't be in uniform yourself then?'

I shook my head. 'It's not that sort of job.'

'It usually isn't,' said Mary resignedly.

Mrs Broyles triumphed over limited resources to produce a dinner of kedgeree with watercress accompanied by an assortment of cold meats, cheese, pickles and salad.

At the table Jaikie appeared quite shy in Mary's company and had little to say for himself. I had the impression that he possessed more information than had been vouchsafed to me and was keeping tight-lipped to avoid any possible slip. However, by the time we got to the bread and butter pudding, Mary had charmed him into revealing some of his earlier adventures. He had spent time on Baffin Island trading in walrus ivory, worked as a deck hand on a trawler, circumnavigated Sicily in a canoe, and made a hiking tour of the Tyrole.

'For the past couple of years,' he concluded, 'I've been employed as an agent of the National Antiquities Council, tracking down lost artefacts and escorting archaeological expeditions around some of the trickier corners of the globe.'

'Good heavens, you're quite the wanderer!' said Mary. 'Haven't you ever considered settling down?'

'Oh, I know exactly where I'm going to settle down,'

Jaikie replied with a flat seriousness usually found only in children. 'I'm just not ready for it yet.'

I felt that behind that statement was a story or two he had left out of his dinner conversation.

Reminding me that we were to be off at first light, he bade us a good night and retired to one of the spare bedrooms. I told Mary what I could of what was up and then we too turned in.

Once up in our bedroom, she opened a drawer and took out something which she then pressed into my hand. It was a small, worn book, the very copy of John Bunyan's *The Pilgrim's Progress* which I had inherited from my old friend Peter Pienaar. Peter had died in 1918 in aerial combat with the German ace Lensch, sacrificing his life to bring the German down and save my division from complete destruction.

He had little enough to pass on, but nothing was more precious to him than this. I kept the book in my desk at Fosse Manor, so that it would always be near at hand, and many was the evening I had soothed my restlessness by reading of Christian's journey to the Celestial City.

I stroked the ragged cover of the book with its faded depiction of the Heavenly Realm, and when my eyes met Mary's I saw that hers were grave and deep.

'But how . . . ?' I began.

'I've been carrying it with me,' she explained. 'You may laugh at this, but I had an intuition that we wouldn't be returning home together and that you would be called away. I knew you would want Peter's book with you when you go into battle.'

'I wouldn't trade it for the world's best rifle,' I said. 'Somehow you're always one step ahead of me.'

'That's because I've always been your future,' she said, touching a hand to my cheek. 'I was before we met and I will be when you return.'

We spent the night pressed close together, aware that it might be some time before we could do so again. The sun had barely cracked the sky before we were up and dressed, bolting down a simple breakfast of eggs and toast with a few cups of strong coffee.

'We'll be going in a few minutes,' said Jaikie with a glance at his wrist watch. He stood by the window, toying with an unlit cigarette.

Though nothing about him suggested a military background, he clearly had experience of tight operations and close teamwork which did not come from anything as innocent as sports.

'We're not going by motorcycle, are we?' I asked. 'One ride like that is enough to last me.'

'No, sir, that's been taken already by two men bearing an uncanny resemblance to the both of us. They are travelling towards Scotland even as we speak and word has leaked out that they're on their way to a secret assignment in Norway.'

'Norway?'

'You've operated there before, sir, and it's as far from our actual destination as can be. Our transport will be arriving any moment now.'

As though it had been summoned by his words, I heard a vehicle pull up outside. It was a small white van with the name of a local firm of plumbers painted on its side. Two men in overalls got out and came up to the front door with bags of tools in their hands. As soon as Jaikie let them in they removed their overalls and passed them over to us. Once Jaikie and I had pulled these on over our normal clothes, they handed us their bags and wished us good luck. Mary gave me a final kiss as Jaikie and I headed out the door and into the van, the keys of which had been left in the ignition.

Jaikie took the wheel and drove off northwards with his eyes as much on the rear-view mirror as the road ahead. The surrounding city was still largely asleep, its long streets deserted apart from a few early-rising tradesmen and newsagents.

'I've played some parts in the past,' I said, 'but I believe this is the first time I've passed myself off as a plumber. I just hope nobody expects me to mend a broken pipe, because they'll be in for a flood if they do.'

'It's only for a short while until we reach our rendezvous point,' Jaikie informed me. His eyes flicked towards the mirror.

'Do you think anyone is following us?' I asked.

'If they are, they must be literally invisible. Still, it never hurts to take precautions.'

I had the tool bag in my lap and when I opened it I saw nestled among the rods and spanners a shoulder holster housing a Webley .38 revolver. When I lifted the weapon out, Jaikie said, 'You can put that on when we stop. There's a box of cartridges in there too.'

We drove past Regent's Park and on to the outskirts of Highgate where we pulled inside a dingy-looking garage. The doors were shut behind us by two men who collected our discarded overalls. Another man dressed in a plain grey suit and cap beckoned us towards a waiting Bentley. Though he was in civvies, he gave us a stiff military salute as we got into the back seats. Here each of us found a small knapsack containing extra clothing and some basic toiletries.

Once our driver was behind the wheel, the other two men rolled up a steel shutter at the far side of the garage and we moved off through this rear exit.

'This is quite the shell game,' I remarked.

'As a youngster in Glasgow,' said Jaikie, 'and an undersized one at that, I became pretty sharp at dodging pursuit by a gang or, on some occasions, the police.'

'I've had to dodge both in my time as well, so I appreciate your expertise.'

Within the hour we had left London behind and were wending our way through the green level fields and tame woodlands of Middlesex. The light broadened steadily as our silent driver steered an unerring course along back roads and country tracks.

Jaikie pulled out a crumpled pack of Virginia cigarettes and offered me one. When I waved it away he popped it into his mouth and lit it, his brow crinkling in thought as he did so.

I slipped *The Pilgrim's Progress* out of my pocket and opened it to the first page of the narrative. Here I read the words:

> *Moreover, I am for certain informed that this our city will be burned by fire from heaven; in which fearful overthrow both myself, with thee my wife, and you*

my sweet babes, shall miserably come to ruin, except (the which yet I see not) some way of escape may be found whereby we may yet be delivered.

These hard words might well be addressed to our own times. Yet I knew that Christian and his family did escape destruction, so there was hope for us as well.

When Jaikie's eye lighted on the book I explained that it had belonged to Peter Pienaar, my mentor during my days in South Africa, who had joined me on some of my European escapades. He was a flier in the war but was shot down over Germany and held prisoner for several months. He passed much of that time reading the Bible and this book, sending me regular letters filled with his reflections on both.

He was eventually released as it was thought his injuries made it impossible for him to serve any further, but he proved everyone wrong, perishing in one final, vital mission.

'Mary has been keeping it close by for me in case I should suddenly be called off on a caper like this,' I said. 'Just leafing through the pages makes me feel that my old friend and my wife are both here with me.' I gave an embarrassed laugh. 'You must think I'm an old sentimentalist.'

'Not at all, sir. As it happens, I have a token from my lady too.'

From his pocket he produced a light brown feather flecked with black.

'That belongs to a kestrel, doesn't it?' I guessed.

'As a matter of fact it belongs to an even finer bird,' said Jaikie proudly. 'To Miss Alison Westwater who entrusted it to me for luck and as a token of her affection. She says that as I long as I hold on to this, I'll always find my way back to her.'

'She sounds like a remarkable young woman. Why haven't you married her?'

Jaikie shifted uncomfortably. 'I can't do that yet, not until I've performed a great deed.'

'And what might that be? Slay a dragon? Pull a magic sword out of a stone?'

Abashed by my gentle mockery, he said, 'I don't know, but I've been in training for years so that when the time comes I'll not be found wanting.'

In my own youth I too fancied I had all the time in the world and thought adventuring and soldiering were the best things life had to offer. Now I knew better.

'Take an old man's advice,' I said, 'and don't wait around for destiny to take a hand. As soon as we get back from this venture you get that girl to a church.'

Jaikie finished his cigarette and sat in silence until we entered Suffolk. A plane was waiting to take us to France and I assumed we were headed for an RAF base. Our actual destination came as a surprise.

'Why, this is a race track,' I declared.

'Newmarket race track to be exact,' said Jaikie, taking some mild enjoyment from my surprise. 'The RAF are using one of the grass strips here as a runway. The great advantage, of course, is that this is an airfield the Germans won't find on any of their maps. Ideal for a clandestine operation like this.'

Skirting the main gate, the driver took us round to a secondary entrance adjoining the main grandstand.

At the northeast end of the enclosure we pulled up by a clubhouse where two men in suits and hats were waiting. As soon as we exited the vehicle they took our places and the car pulled off, heading back towards the main road.

Jaikie checked his watch again in obvious expectation.

'Don't tell me we have to ride horses next,' I joked.

'It's not come to that,' said a voice from the open door of the clubhouse.

A moment later a familiar figure stepped into view.

7

THE FLIGHT OF THE
BLESSED ANTONIA

'Archie Roylance!' I exclaimed at the sight of my old friend.

In spite of the injury to his leg, which had plagued him for years, Archie approached us with a jaunty spring in his step. He was dressed in a flying suit with an RAF crest.

'Dick,' he greeted me cheerily, 'I knew it was only a matter of time before you'd be off on some wild caper. It's a pretty kettle of fish this time around, eh?'

As a young man Sir Archibald Roylance had been one of my subalterns in the old Lennox Highlanders until he left to join the Flying Corps. After the war he took up politics and diplomacy until he sickened of both and retired to his Scottish estate.

We exchanged hearty handshakes.

'Archie, I thought they had you busy training new pilots.'

'That's right,' Archie affirmed airily, 'but they can't keep me from sneaking back into action whenever the mood takes me. And I certainly wasn't going to let some sprog who's still wet behind the ears fly General Sir Richard Hannay into the middle of this set-to.'

He shifted his attention to my companion and his face lit up.

'And bless me if it isn't John Galt. How have you been, Jaikie? I haven't seen you since that time you turned my pleasant Austrian jaunt into a king-sized pickle.'

Jaikie raised a cautioning hand, as if to keep Archie from saying anything further about that particular incident. 'You know how it is, Sir Archie. I've been doing a bit of this, a bit of that.'

With an effort Archie stifled his Austrian reminiscences and regarded us with a broad grin, as though we were a pair of comic entertainers. 'I swear I never met two chaps with such a talent for getting in and out of the hairiest scrapes. Dick, I first met Jaikie here when he was only a sprat.'

'I remember it well,' said Jaikie.

'Back in those days you were one of that gang of ragamuffins old McCunn took under his wing. What did you call yourselves again? The Glasgow Divers, wasn't it?'

'Die-Hards,' Jaikie corrected him. 'The Gorbals Die-Hards. And we weren't a gang. We couldn't afford the cost of a uniform to join the Boy Scouts, so the six of us formed our own troop.'

Archie nodded sagely. 'Yes, I remember now. Had your own flag and everything. So what became of the rest of the Divers?'

Jaikie didn't bother to correct him again. 'Oh, some of them are still around,' he replied enigmatically.

'Well, chaps, any further reminiscing will have to wait,' said Archie, leading us towards a camouflaged hangar. 'I don't know exactly what you're up to, but I do know I've to fetch you over to France before the day's much older.'

'You've received the flight plan, Sir Archie?' Jaikie enquired.

'Absolutely, Jaikie, maps and all. Though why you

should want to be dropped off near some obscure French château is a bit of a poser.'

When we entered the hangar I saw a plane scarcely larger than a fighter with its wings set unusually high. Two mechanics in oil-stained coveralls were just finishing their pre-flight ground checks. They stepped away as we approached and one of them wiped his face with a rag.

'We've done all we can, sir,' he told Archie. 'I reckon she's as close to airworthy now as she'll ever be.'

'I'm sure she'll do, Harry,' said Archie. 'I'm quite sure of that.'

The grey fuselage was marked with the familiar roundel of the RAF while the tail fin bore the tricolour of our French allies. More striking were the words painted in bright red beneath the pilot's cockpit: *The Blessed Antonia*.

'She's a Westland Lysander,' Archie told us proudly, 'a grand old bus, and, as you can see, I've named her after my dear old Aunt Antonia.'

'Would it be impolite to ask why?' Jaikie hazarded.

'Not at all,' Archie responded jovially. 'You see, when I was a boy, my sisters and I often spent the summer months with my Aunt Antonia, who was actually a cousin of my father once removed. Or maybe it was twice. Anyway, through all the months we spent with her during those childhood years, she never once let us down.'

Archie gave the plane an affectionate pat as he continued his story, almost as if his aunt were actually embodied in the aircraft.

'If she had promised us a day at the beach, then off to the beach we would go, no matter if there was a gale blowing and rain lashing down. If she had promised us crumpets for tea, then crumpets there would be, even if she had to use the sharp end of her most dangerous umbrella to compel the baker to whip up a fresh batch. That's why I've always referred to her as the Blessed Antonia.'

For a moment Archie's eyes became misty, as though he were seeing again these scenes from his childhood. Then, recollecting himself, he ran his finger along the painted letters. 'I decided that if I gave the same name to this venerable crate then she also would never let me down. And believe me, she's already got me out of one or two tight spots.'

'That much is obvious,' I observed, noting that there were at least a dozen bullet holes marking the body of the plane.

'Yes, she took a few hits during the Dunkirk operation,' Archie acknowledged ruefully, 'but she brought me back safe and sound every time.'

'It looks pretty cramped in there,' said Jaikie, peering into the passenger cockpit.

'She was originally designed to carry only a single passenger,' said Archie, 'but she's been modified to squeeze in two, provided neither one is on the stout side. Plus she only needs a short runway for take-off and landing. If need be, I swear I could bring her down on a tennis court.'

Archie climbed into the pilot's seat and strapped on his helmet. I clambered into the passenger cockpit with Jaikie cramming in behind me. It occurred to me that, as well as his other qualifications, his ability to fit himself into such a narrow space might be another reason Blenkiron had selected him for this particular assignment. I had to loosen my shoulder holster and slide it around to keep the pistol from digging into my ribs and I could feel Jaikie squirming about behind me in quest of the least uncomfortable position.

Once our helmets were on and the cockpit closed, the ground crew cleared the chocks from under the wheels. The engine coughed into life and we rolled slowly out of the hangar. The two mechanics waved their farewells and one of them shook his head as though amazed we had made it even this far. Turning left, we taxied onto a flat stretch of green running parallel to the race track and began our take-off run. The roar of the engine and the whirr of the propeller rose to a high pitch as we gathered speed. With thirty feet of grass to spare, Archie deftly adjusted the stick and we lifted off the ground as gently as a feather swept up in a breeze.

It was so long since I had been up in a plane that I had almost forgotten the sheer exhilaration of flight. To see the earth dropping away below and the clouds rushing down on us from the azure sky made me feel as if all the heavy cares of the world were as insubstantial as a morning mist. We banked southwards, passing over a chequerboard of fields, with the sea a distant gleam to our left.

Archie had grown up around horses and his expertise as a rider had translated seamlessly into the skills of a pilot. However, like many an experienced horseman, he had a preference for the spirited sort of mount that offered a more challenging ride, and this had carried over into a particular liking for a more cantankerous aircraft. I heard the engine give an occasional splutter and I was sure that not every bump and jolt was due to the air currents.

Archie seemed to delight in these slight difficulties, handling the plane with the sure, light touch of a horseman coaxing his mount over a series of high fences. From the few unhappy grunts he was unable to suppress I guessed that Jaikie had never flown with Archie before and did not have the same confidence in his piloting skills that I had acquired in the last war.

As we passed over the Thames Archie swooped down to give us a view of the various vessels, both military and civilian, that were busily plying the waters. Off to our right a sooty smudge hung over the distant smokestacks of London and an RAF transport plane passed over us on its way to the city.

'One of the new Bristol Bombays,' Archie informed us over the radio. 'Not a patch on the old Handley Page planes if you ask me.'

We flew over the once peaceful fields of Kent, now dotted with an array of early warning stations. Where once beacons would have been lit on the hilltops, now telephones and radios stood manned and ready to warn of an enemy attack.

As we skirted the coast I looked down on the choppy waters of the Channel. A Royal Navy cruiser and a smaller vessel, perhaps a fishing boat, were paralleling each other on a westward course. Most of our troops had been successfully pulled off the beaches, but I knew that some of our men were still making their way to the coast in dribs and drabs and the navy was on the lookout for any of them attempting to cross by rowboat or dinghy.

A sudden gust of wind struck us broadside, causing the *Blessed Antonia* to crow-hop sideways like a skittish horse. Jaikie let out an involuntary yelp.

'Don't worry, Jaikie,' I assured him. 'Sir Archie has got me through much worse than this.'

'I don't think I have much of a stomach for flying,' Jaikie confessed. 'To tell you the truth, I'd feel more at home on one of those boats down there.'

'Not a bit of it, Jaikie,' Archie called back cheerfully. 'Safe as houses up here. Let me give you a few lessons and you'll be as merry in a plane as you would be on the back of your favourite mare.'

'Actually, sir, I'm not much of a horseman either.'

'On your favourite bicycle then,' Archie amended. 'You take my word for it.'

Below us the lush green of Romney Marsh gave way to the bleached shingle of Dungeness. Here we parted company with England and struck out over open water with our own shadow chasing us across the waves.

As we closed on the French coast my earlier mood of pleasurable excitement was soon replaced by that quickening of the pulse and the prickle in my scalp that I always felt in the moments before a battle. This was hostile territory ahead, overrun by an enemy now more ruthless and coldly determined than ever before.

Rugged white cliffs reared before us, split by a broad river flowing out into the sea. At the base of the cliffs a seaside town straddled the estuary, its shops and houses as brightly painted as toys. An assortment of small boats bobbed at anchor inside a stone breakwater. Everything appeared peaceful but I felt as though a palpable chill had crept into the air.

Archie's thoughts must have been running parallel with mine. 'Our planes have all been pulled out of France,' he said, 'in spite of the promises Churchill gave to support them. Still, what choice did we have, eh? If France goes down, we'll need every crate we can scrape up for the next battle.'

'You mean the invasion?' I said. 'Surely we can hold the Channel against them.'

'Not if they're free to bomb the blazes out of our defences,' said Archie. 'No, the thing will be decided in the sky, you mark my words.'

I couldn't tell whether this was an accurate assessment of the situation or merely sprang from Archie's personal enthusiasm for air power.

'Of course some of our chaps are still flying reccies over here,' Archie resumed, 'and even lending a hand where they can, whatever their orders. It's hard to tell if the French are glad to see them or are resentful of our supposed betrayal – you know, perfidious Albion and all that rot.'

'I suppose our own reception is just as unpredictable,' said Jaikie.

Years ago I had flown with Archie as an observer, spying out the enemy positions, and I found myself almost unconsciously slipping back into that role, noting bridges, crossroads and other vital points on the ground below. I spotted a body of men moving in column to the east and reported this to Archie. 'I can't make out which side they belong to,' I told him.

'Good,' said Archie. 'That means they can't tell who we are either.'

Even so, he brought us down to fifteen hundred feet to lessen the risk of our being silhouetted against the open sky. Skirting the town of Blangy, we followed a railway line southwards. Suddenly a booming series of smoky detonations darkened the sky to our left.

'Don't bother about that,' Archie scoffed. 'Just Jerry chancing a few pot shots. Of course, once they get their ack-ack properly set up, it will be a different story.'

I continued to keep a sharp lookout, which was why I was the first to spot the incoming planes.

'Bogeys at ten o'clock,' I informed Archie.

There were three of them, well above our height and moving fast. As they drew nearer Archie squinted up at them.

'Rest easy,' he said. 'That's one of our lads in a Hurricane leading the way.'

'And the two following him?' Jaikie wondered.

As the British plane passed over us we saw the gun-metal grey of his pursuers and the distinctive crosses marking their wings. Both of them loosed off a volley of machine-gun fire at their quarry.

'Messerschmitts,' Archie grunted in a tone he usually reserved for ill-mannered guests who were spoiling a party.

The Hurricane pilot banked right and soared skywards out of range. One of the Messerschmitts followed him, guns still blazing. The other German peeled off and circled back towards us. He was in no apparent hurry, confident that we were easy prey.

'Is this plane armed, sir?' Jaikie enquired in a matter-of-fact tone. 'I didn't notice any weaponry.'

Now that danger was upon us, rather than anticipated, he exhibited the same calm alertness that had struck me as so impressive during our adventure in London.

'Afraid not,' Archie apologised. 'We had to chuck the guns in order to fit in an extra passenger and the larger fuel tank. Rather hoped we wouldn't run into a scrap.'

'Can we outrun him?' I asked.

'Not a chance,' said Archie. 'But not to worry. I've got a few tricks to throw at him.'

The Messerschmitt was closing fast on our right flank, lining up to rake us from nose to tail. Archie gave a determined growl. 'Hang on, chaps,' he warned us. 'Things are about to get bumpy.'

8

A SPORTING CHANCE

———

Even as the enemy pilot unleashed a stream of bullets Archie threw us into a steep corkscrew dive. Taken by surprise, the German's own momentum carried him past us as we spun towards the ground like a Catherine wheel.

Green meadows rushed up to meet us until, at what felt like the last possible instant, *Antonia* levelled out. The next thing I knew, we were back on course and rapidly gaining altitude.

Archie was keenly surveying the landscape, in search of I knew not what. It seemed to me that our only chance of survival was to continue dodging the enemy pilot until he ran out of ammunition – a very slim chance indeed.

'I take it, Archie, you have some sort of plan in mind?' I suggested as mildly as I could.

'Working on it, old man, working on it,' Archie assured me.

He made a quarter turn and increased speed towards a ridge of high ground a few miles off. Jaikie kept watch astern and reported that the German was working his way back towards us.

'Let's give him something to think about.' Archie sounded confident.

We sped for the ridge at full throttle and as we crested the summit we went into a swan dive. The *Blessed Antonia* swooped down the reverse slope while the German overshot us again, spitting out a fruitless salvo as he passed.

'Now,' said Archie, as though resuming his earlier train of thought, 'your German flier has two outstanding qualities: pride and determination. With a spot of luck I may be able to use both of those against him.'

A rugged, wooded valley opened up ahead of us. Outlined briefly against the sun, the Messerschmitt executed a barrel roll and bore down on us again like a ravenous bird of prey.

'He's certainly persistent,' I remarked.

'He knows if he stays up too high he might lose sight of us,' said Archie. 'But the closer we both are to the ground, the less he can use his speed against us.'

He raced *Antonia* up the valley as though he were guiding a horse on a steeplechase, taking advantage of every trough and hillock to throw the German off our tail. I could sense the tips of the tallest trees brushing against the undercarriage, as though Archie were deliberately making the manoeuvre as hazardous as possible.

'More importantly,' he continued, 'he has to prove that he can match me. You're about to see how determined he is to do that.'

'Would that have anything to do with those dangerous obstacles up ahead?' Jaikie wondered.

I too was staring at the two tall outcrops of stone rising up like twin pillars out of the sea of trees.

'Spot on, Jaikie,' Archie approved. 'You see, I told you I could make a flier out of you.'

The gap ahead looked barely wide enough for our wingspan, and I couldn't help but think of the fabled

Clashing Rocks through which Jason had to steer his vessel without being smashed by their grinding jaws. Though I was pretty sure these rocks wouldn't budge, our danger was increased by the fact that Archie had to waggle the plane from side to side to evade the bursts of machine-gun fire now coming directly from our rear. He muttered a few ungentlemanly words as several bullets struck home with a sound like hailstones beating on a window.

I braced myself for disaster, but Archie kept us on course and we shot through the crags with only inches to spare. A rattle of gunfire behind us sent rock splinters flying and the Messerschmitt burst into view, her wings still intact.

The terrain before us broadened out into farmland. A village lay directly in our path, a jumble of roofs encircling a medieval church. The lofty spire was crowned with a wrought-iron weather vane in the form of a cockerel.

'That looks promising,' said Archie, making a beeline for it.

As we approached the spire, he swung *Antonia* abruptly around on her starboard wing, whipping us around the church in a tight arc. The manoeuvre put the tower between us and our pursuer just as he loosed off a stream of bullets that smacked the weather vane and sent it into a crazy spin.

I thought for an instant the Messerschmitt might collide with the building but the pilot pulled her clear and roared angrily skywards in search of a fresh angle of attack.

Archie headed southeast across country that was banded with woodland. The German was not long in joining us, matching us speed for speed. To my surprise he didn't open fire. 'Do you suppose his gun's jammed?' I wondered.

Archie shook his head. 'He's low on ammo so he's saving whatever's left for a clear shot. We need to shake him off before he gets one.'

We bobbed and weaved across the countryside then Archie exclaimed, 'Is that a river over there?'

I could see a glint of silver in the distance off to our left. 'I believe you're right.'

'Well, that's just the ticket,' Archie declared, altering course towards it.

The distant glimmer quickly expanded into a broad river flowing between steep embankments.

'We're not going to splash down, are we?' Jaikie asked.

'Not a bit of it,' said Archie dismissively. 'Where there's a river, there's bound to be a bridge.'

We dropped to within a few feet of the water and held tightly to its course as though we were following a road. The German stayed doggedly on our tail. After a mile or two we swung round a bend and saw ahead the very bridge Archie was hoping for.

It was a modern affair, a utilitarian construction of steel set upon squat concrete pilings. Whistling tunelessly between his teeth, Archie aimed us directly at the space between the two central piers.

'Archie, you can't be serious,' I breathed.

'Never more so,' he responded jovially.

Our enemy was coming up behind, as unshakeable as a shadow.

'Why doesn't he finish us?' asked Jaikie. 'Surely he won't get a better shot than this.'

'As a fellow pilot he can see what I'm attempting,' Archie laughed, 'and it wouldn't be sporting to interfere. He wants to see if we can make it.'

'I'm quite interested in the result myself,' I said.

I confess there was a desperate prayer on my lips as that low horizontal slot came rushing towards us with the inexorable menace of a speeding train. It looked so cramped that any attempt to pass through must surely send us ploughing into the river.

Then, at the most extreme instant, Archie deftly tilted our wings to the right and we shot through, lightly skimming the water below us. For a moment we were in shadow, then we burst out into the sunlight, alive and exultant.

I twisted round just in time to see the German pursuing us relentlessly into the same gap. His obstinate pride proved to be his doom. His left wing tip struck the edge of the stonework, whipping the plane over in a violent cartwheel. It crashed against brick, steel and water then burst apart in a flash of flame and spark-filled smoke.

Archie coasted back to review the wreckage and shook his head sadly.

'He was a gallant foe,' he said. 'It's a damned shame.'

'He certainly had guts,' Jaikie agreed.

'Sometimes,' I reflected, 'even the worst of causes can be served by the very best of men.'

'Here comes another one!' Jaikie exclaimed.

Another plane was swooping down on us, but Archie

gave a chuckle of relief. 'Nothing to worry about. It's our old friend in the Hurricane.'

Noting the remains of the downed Messerschmitt, the RAF man passed close enough for us to see the smile on his face as he gave us a triumphant thumbs-up. Archie returned the gesture and the Hurricane veered off in the direction of the Channel.

'He must have dealt with his Messerschmitt too,' I said.

'Very decent of him to come and check on us,' said Archie. 'He'll have barely enough fuel to get home now.'

Our elation over our escape was suddenly displaced by a more pressing concern. The engine stuttered and the plane began to dip and sway.

'She's been pretty badly shot up,' said Archie through gritted teeth. 'Come on, old girl, up you go.'

The *Blessed Antonia* fought gamely to regain a measure of lift, but I could hear the engine labouring.

'We need a place to set down,' Archie informed us. 'I'll gain as much height as I can, so that if she cuts out on us, we'll be able to glide for a while.'

I could see from the way he was struggling with the controls that he had his work cut out for him saving our necks.

'Jerry's shredded some of the control lines,' he grunted, 'and the engine's taken a knock too.'

We passed over two ranks of poplar trees lining a country road beyond which lay open pastureland.

The propeller was only going by fits and starts and the engine was squealing and grinding as we swooped towards the ground at an alarming rate. We jolted down in a ploughed field with a series of bumps that set my teeth shaking. The *Blessed Antonia* rattled and creaked to a jarring halt that jerked us all forward in our seats.

Archie's voice sounded urgently. 'Out we get! There's a chance the fuel tank might blow!'

Struggling free of our harnesses, we wrestled open the hood of the cockpit and scrambled out. Two strides from the plane Archie stumbled and fell. Jaikie and I snatched him up by the elbows and carried him with us to a safe distance. Behind us *Antonia*'s damaged engine gave up the fight and died.

We paused for breath, leaning against a freestone wall. Archie grimaced in pain. Pulling himself together, he said, 'Sorry, chaps, my dratted leg's gone on me again.'

I clapped him on the shoulder. 'At least we're all in one piece.'

Jaikie's eyes were aglow with the sheer delight of being alive. Patting his pocket, he gave us a lopsided grin. 'I'm not the superstitious type,' he said, 'but I can't help feeling this lucky feather of Alison's had something to do with us getting down safely.'

'I'm ready to credit anything from lucky charms to angels,' I said, 'but I think it's mostly down to our pilot.'

Archie waved the tribute away. 'Think nothing of it, Dick. Just basic flying, that's all.'

He tried to take a step but pulled up short with a groan of pain.

'Just take a few minutes,' I advised him.

'I don't think we have a few minutes,' said Jaikie.

With a nod of his head he directed our attention to a figure striding towards us across the field. It was a burly farmer in rustic clothing, a wide straw hat and heavy boots, carrying a double-barrelled shotgun. I was aware of the pistol under my jacket, but I decided against drawing it. We wouldn't get far if we made enemies of the locals and, after all, we were trespassing on his land.

The farmer levelled his shotgun and glared at us. His attitude was none too welcoming and I reflected that Archie might have been right about the ambiguous reception that would await us among our French allies.

Halting a few paces away, he demanded truculently, 'Qu'est-ce que vous faites ici? Vous êtes anglais?'

Archie was in uniform, but Jaikie and I were in civvies, an incongruity that prompted the Frenchman to regard us with deep suspicion. The worrying thought occurred to me that perhaps the Germans had already overrun this stretch of country and that this man had thrown his lot in with his new masters.

I was still trying to formulate a response when Jaikie took a small, unthreatening step forward. A smile of childlike innocence touched his lips. He pointed at the tricolour on our tail fin then tapped himself on the chest.

'Je suis écossais.'

'Écossais?' the farmer repeated quizzically. He did not lower his shotgun but did appear affected by this reminder of the ancient ties of the Auld Alliance.

In the most basic French Jaikie explained to him that we had been brought down in aerial combat but that we had destroyed our German enemy. Then he initiated the universal gesture of wartime friendship. He took out his crumpled pack of cigarettes and offered one to the farmer.

After a momentary hesitation the Frenchman

accepted it. He lowered his shotgun and leaned forward so that Jaikie could give him a light. Resting the weapon in the crook of his arm, he took a long draw and gestured at the plane. He told us the Germans were in the area and if this were spotted we would all be for the chop.

'Look, if we can get her out of sight,' said Archie, 'I might be able to fix her up.'

Jaikie and I discussed our problem with our new friend and he offered a solution. With the help of a mule, a carthorse and some tackle, he dragged the plane out of the mud while we pushed it from behind. After twenty minutes of strenuous manoeuvring the *Blessed Antonia* found a home in a barn behind the farmhouse.

'I can see a bright future for you as a diplomat,' I complimented Jaikie.

'Just as well it worked,' he said. 'That was my last cigarette.'

The Frenchman invited us into his kitchen. Here his wife, a squat, blunt-faced woman, stood at the stove intently stirring a pot of stew. She fixed a wary eye on us and kept a large, well-sharpened kitchen knife close to hand. Her husband gave her a silent signal that all was well but her stirring did not slow and her eye lost none of its watchfulness.

Two boys of around ten and twelve sat rigidly at the table, clearly following orders to remain silent and out of the way. The farmer assured his children that they had nothing to fear from us and they visibly relaxed. Then he brought out four unwashed glasses and poured a splash of wine into each. Raising his own he called out defiantly, 'À la victoire!'

We joined him in the toast, though at this point it seemed a forlorn hope. Once we had swallowed our wine Archie headed for the door.

'I'm going to give *Antonia* a good look over and see what can be done.'

As he limped outside I tried to recollect the French words for painkillers so that I could ask the farmer for some relief for our friend. He was pouring us each a second glass when there came the roar of an engine from outside.

Jaikie darted to the window and peered out, taking care to keep himself out of sight. A dark frown creased his brow.

'Germans!'

9

THE FALSE PRISONER

———

I joined Jaikie at the window and saw two men on motorcycles roaring up the road towards the yard. They were both dressed in the distinctive grey uniforms of the Wehrmacht. Even if he had seen them in time, Archie, with his bad leg, had no chance of getting out of sight. They spotted him at once and drew up their bikes on either side of him, unslinging their submachine guns.

'Outriders sent ahead to scout for enemy positions and sources of supply,' I surmised.

The farmer and his wife immediately moved to where their children were seated and placed protective hands on their shoulders.

Jaikie reached under his jacket for his pistol. 'We need to get out there.'

'Yes, but not like that,' I cautioned him. 'If we run out, guns blazing, Archie will be the first to take a bullet.'

I don't think of myself as an especially brainy sort of fellow, but in times of crisis my thoughts seem to shift into a higher gear and ideas sometimes come to me with almost dazzling speed.

'Look, I've got a notion that just might come off,' I told Jaikie. 'You need to take off your jacket and shirt.'

In as few words as possible I explained the gist of my plan and Jaikie swiftly followed my instructions. Both of us discarded our shoulder holsters and, as a final touch,

I borrowed the farmer's hat and clapped it on my head. The two of us stepped outside, Jaikie in his vest and I in my shirt sleeves.

The closer of the two Germans, a sergeant, had dismounted and was poking Archie in the belly with his gun. Archie had both hands raised and was proclaiming in English that he did not understand the questions being barked at him in German.

'Sorry, old man, no savvy the lingo,' he declared as though addressing a difficult foreign waiter.

They had noticed he was headed towards the barn and the other rider drove his bike there while keeping one eye over his shoulder. It was at this point that they spotted Jaikie and me coming out of the cottage.

I had Jaikie's right arm pinned behind his back in a hammerlock while my left arm was wrapped tightly around his throat. I addressed the Germans in the voice of an indignant Frenchman trying his best to express himself in their tongue.

'These men are spies,' I told them angrily. 'They parachuted in, invaded my house, demanded food, threatened my wife.'

As I spoke Jaikie made a show of trying to break free. In the course of our mock struggle we spun around completely, so that the Germans could see neither of us carried a weapon. The sergeant yelled at me to halt then ordered his companion to investigate the barn.

Archie seized the opportunity to distract the enemy. 'Don't listen to that fellow,' he said, gesturing at me. 'He's talking absolute tosh. I just dropped by to borrow some sugar.'

The sergeant commanded him in obscene terms to keep his mouth shut.

Jaikie was continuing to struggle. His naturally pale features had turned pure white. I knew that meant he was keyed up for action, but to the sergeant it gave him the appearance of a terrified prisoner. The other German got off his bike and with both hands pulled open the barn door.

At the sight of the *Blessed Antonia* he exclaimed, 'Ein Flugzeug!'

The sergeant instinctively glanced over at the plane, taking his attention from me just long enough.

I released my grip on Jaikie and pulled my pistol from the back of his belt, where it had been hidden between our bodies. As the sergeant's eyes swung back to us, Jaikie threw himself flat on the ground. I straightened my arm and fired off three shots into the German's chest. He crumpled in his tracks, the gun dropping from his lifeless fingers. Archie made a grab for it, but his knee gave way beneath him and he sprawled out with a grunt of pain.

The other German made to raise his weapon, but the shoulder strap hooked onto the handlebar of his motorcycle. Abandoning the effort to open fire, he flung himself onto the saddle and kick-started the engine. Even as I took aim, the bike lurched forward and my shot went wide. Seeing he was now outnumbered, the soldier tried to make good his escape.

The farmer, however, had exited the house from the other side and taken cover behind one of the rickety sheds. Now he stepped into view and fired both barrels of his shotgun into the oncoming rider. The German jerked in the saddle and the bike skewed out of control. It smashed into a tree and spilled the rider onto the ground.

I ran over to assure myself that he was no longer a threat. He was plainly dead and the bike was wrecked. The Frenchman joined me and stood over the body.

'They killed my brother at Ypres and now they have come to kill me and my family.' He spat vehemently. 'To the devil with all of them.'

I handed him back his hat and rejoined my two companions. Now that the action was over, the colour was returning to Jaikie's cheeks, but he appeared shaken and poked around in his pockets for a non-existent cigarette.

'Are you all right, Jaikie?' I asked.

'I hope you won't think less of me, sir,' he said gravely. 'I've been through a few scrapes but I'm still not used to seeing a man shot down right in front of me.'

'That's not something we should ever take for granted,' I said. 'They are the enemy, but they're just men after all, and probably not so different from you and me.'

We helped Archie to his feet. He was grinning as he dusted himself off. 'Dick, I've never known such a fellow as you for taking the craziest of chances. He might have shot you both as soon as you walked out.'

'He hadn't shot you, so obviously he wanted information,' I said. 'I reckoned he'd hesitate just long enough for us to get the drop on him. It was Jaikie who was really in harm's way.'

'All I had to do was hit the deck without spoiling your shot,' Jaikie said modestly.

'How much of a start do you suppose these chaps have on the rest of their gang?' Archie wondered.

'These bikes move pretty fast, so probably at least an hour,' I guessed. 'It doesn't look as if they're meeting much resistance.'

'Well, I'd best get on with tending the blessed old girl,' said Archie, limping off to the barn.

While he made his inspection of the *Blessed Antonia*, Jaikie and I helped the farmer dump the bodies in a disused well behind the chicken coop. Before stashing the broken bike under some bales of hay we siphoned the petrol out of its tank and used it to top up the other motorcycle.

We returned to the kitchen long enough to wolf down some soup and crusty bread while the lady of the house took a snack out for Archie to nibble on while he worked. Once we were outside again the farmer told us he was going to load up his wagon and get the family out of here before the Germans overran the whole country.

Jaikie cast an anxious look at the sky. 'We'd best get moving too. There's only a couple of hours of daylight left.'

According to the farmer, the nearest town of any size was Gisors. Armed with this information, we joined Archie for a council of war, spreading our map across the plane's nose. With the tip of his finger Jaikie traced out our proposed route to the Château du Cygne where we were to join the rest of the team Blenkiron had assembled for this mission.

'I reckon with that bike we could make it there before nightfall,' he said.

'Only two of us could ride on it,' I pointed out.

Archie clapped me on the shoulder. 'Never mind about me,' he said in his bluffest voice. 'Even if I could come along, I would only slow you down with this leg of mine. No, you go on ahead and I'll stay here with *Antonia*.'

'But supposing you can't get her up again?'

'I told you,' said Archie with spirited confidence, 'that she'll never let me down. She got us this far, didn't she? In spite of the best efforts of the Luftwaffe. Look, the chances are no Jerries will come poking around until morning. By that time I can have her back in tip-top condition and be in the air by sunrise.'

'Do you think you can make it back to England?' Jaikie asked.

'I'll give it a darned good try,' Archie replied. 'With any luck I'll catch up with you chaps further down the road, some place where there aren't quite so many Huns trying to kill us.'

We made our farewells and I climbed onto the German motorcycle behind Jaikie.

'A BMW R35 with four-stroke single-cylinder engine,' he said admiringly. 'I can't say I'm sorry to get my hands on one of these.'

'I seem to be spending an awful lot of time as a passenger,' I sighed ruefully.

'Don't worry about it,' said Jaikie. 'Just relax and enjoy the ride.'

Leaning against his beloved plane, Archie gave a jaunty wave as Jaikie started the bike and we roared off. I hailed our French friend as we passed him loading a last suitcase onto his horse-drawn wagon. He turned and cried out, 'Bonne chance!' in return, waving his fist in the air.

We followed an earthen track that took us through the nearest village. Here also, the remaining inhabitants were packing up their belongings to flee. Many cottages already stood deserted and in their abandoned gardens the roses and lilies drooped as if in mourning.

Beyond the village we crossed a train track pitted with craters, the rail lines broken and twisted by a well-aimed bomb. In a nearby field lay the mangled corpse of a bull, an innocent victim of the bombardment.

When we reached the main road we were forced to join a slow-moving stream of displaced civilians. Everything into which a few precious belongings could be loaded formed part of the unhappy procession: wagons, carts, prams and wheelbarrows, all accompanied by women, children and old men.

Only the women held their heads high, strong in the midst of hardship. This was their great virtue, to comfort their children when they were afraid and give courage to their men when they were downcast. I was reminded that it was from such stock as this that Joan of Arc arose to lead France back from defeat.

There were bicycles weaving among the crowd as well as trucks and cars grinding their gears in frustration at the pace. Many vehicles had run out of fuel and been abandoned, creating further obstacles to the already stuttering progress.

'We're getting nowhere at this rate,' I heard Jaikie murmur over the rumble of the motorcycle engine.

I was about to agree with him when I was interrupted by a series of shrill cries behind me. I twisted around and saw the cause – a single plane streaking down from the sky. As it plunged, the siren fixed to its undercarriage screeched like a demented banshee.

'Stuka!' came the horrified cry down the line as people crouched behind their vehicles or flung themselves onto the ground.

Jaikie whipped us over onto the roadside and we threw ourselves flat as the aircraft came screaming overhead. From the brief glimpse I caught, it had already unloaded its bomb and was saving its bullets for a worthwhile target. It disappeared into the haze then came the harsh clatter of machine guns. I wondered whether the pilot had spotted a military vehicle or merely decided there was some strategic purpose to be served by terrorising civilians.

Jaikie hauled the bike back up and we climbed aboard.

'Are you ready for a ride across some rough country?' he asked.

'We certainly can't go on shuffling along like this,' I said. 'Do your worst.'

We pulled away from the road and into a stretch of woodland, bumping over roots and flying across mossy hillocks. Emerging from the trees, we cut a path across a cornfield then startled some sheep from their grazing. Presently we came to a bridge clogged with opposing herds of cattle, their herders clearly in disagreement about which was the direction that led away from the invaders. Without hesitation Jaikie took us directly across the stream, throwing up high sheets of water on either side of us.

'Are you quite sure we're still on the right route?' I asked.

Jaikie nodded. 'I have a sort of instinct about that sort of thing. I couldn't get lost if I tried.'

'In that case, I'll do my best just to enjoy the scenery.'

We finally crested a hill to see a lush vineyard spread out before us and beyond it the white walls and russet rooftops of an elegant château. Jaikie paused to enjoy the sight as the sun set on the distant western hills.

'Let's hope the rest of the lads made it safely,' he said, starting down the slope. Skirting the vineyard, we joined a path that took us onto a broad driveway. As we approached the open gateway the road was immediately blocked by three armed French soldiers who did not look pleased to see us.

10

THE SPECIAL RESERVE

––––

The guards called on us to halt and Jaikie swerved to a stop right in front of them. We dismounted under their sceptical gaze, their rifles following our every move. Not that I could blame them: the fact that we were dressed as civilians and were riding a German military motorcycle made us decidedly suspect.

Jaikie's instructions had specified this as the meeting point between us and the rest of the team, but neither he nor Blenkiron had anticipated that it would be occupied by French soldiers. Given the fluid nature of war, we were lucky, I supposed, not to find it occupied by the Germans.

I explained to the guards that, although I was in civilian garb, I was a British officer and wished to meet with their commander. The trio conferred briefly and it was clear that their orders covered the arrival of reinforcements or an encounter with the enemy, but not this particular situation.

One of them waved us forward and escorted us up the drive with Jaikie pushing the bike along beside him. The well-tended lawn spreading away on both sides had been invaded by cattle who were grazing peacefully, as though all were right with the world.

In stark contrast, even though it was almost dark, there were still men digging trenches and setting up mortar positions around the château. The building itself had the sturdy walls of a medieval fortress with two high turrets from which lookouts were keeping watch over the surrounding country.

Jaikie parked the bike and we climbed the stone steps to a double doorway. The entrance hall was vast, with swords, shields and animal heads arrayed along the walls. Soldiers were dragging sandbags and mattresses over the tiled floor to where they could be used to bolster the windows against a possible bombardment. The guard ushered us up a broad carpeted stairway to an upper gallery decorated with old tapestries of hunting scenes and knights in armour.

We were shown into a spacious study where a young captain stood over a wide desk. He was pointing to a hastily sketched map of the house and grounds while discussing with two subordinates the disposition of their heavy machine guns. Our escort saluted and presented us before being dismissed.

'I am Captain Fabrice Leconte of the Seventh Chasseurs,' the commander told us. 'I did not think there were any English left in France.'

I introduced myself as General Richard Hannay, formerly of the Lennox Highlanders.

'I am John Galt, sir,' said Jaikie, 'a civilian assigned to General Hannay's command.'

'A general?' drawled Leconte. 'You have mislaid your army? Ah yes, they have escaped across la Manche, leaving you behind.' There was amusement in his eyes but an edge of bitterness in his tone.

'We flew from London today,' I informed him with all the politeness I could muster, 'on a mission of the highest importance. We were forced down by the Germans and barely escaped being captured. It has not been an easy journey.'

'No,' said Leconte dispassionately, 'I do not imagine it has. And there are only the two of you?'

'It was planned that the rest of our unit would meet us here.'

Leconte cast an appraising eye over us, as though assessing a pair of new recruits. Though he was no older than Jaikie, he had the air of one whose military lineage stretched all the way back to the days of Napoleon.

'They are already here,' he declared at last. 'They told some story about being separated from their regiment and seeking their commanding officer. It sounded unlikely, no less so even now.'

'I assure you that our mission will in no way interfere with your operations here,' I told him.

'My operation is to hold this château against the Germans to the last bullet,' he informed me. 'What is your business?'

'It is a matter vital to both our nations,' I replied.

The captain raised a sardonic eyebrow. 'And you cannot tell me more than that?'

'I would need to meet my men first,' I said.

'Very well,' said Leconte. 'Bonnet here will take you to them. I will speak with you again when you will perhaps be more . . . conversational?'

His eyes returned to the map and he began making small notations on it in pencil. Corporal Bonnet led us out of the room and down a long carpeted corridor lined with paintings and ornate mirrors. At the far end we were shown into a high-ceilinged, grandly furnished room occupied by three men in the uniform of the Highland Regiment. Their rifles and packs were stacked in the corner while they sat on cushioned chairs playing cards on an ornate Louis XV table.

At the sight of Jaikie they jumped to their feet and rushed to meet him. I judged them all to be slightly older than he, but their obvious delight spoke volumes about the childhood friendship that had forged a lifelong bond between them.

The first to clasp Jaikie's outstretched hand was a burly, red-headed fellow wearing the gold bar of a second lieutenant. He had the rugged face of a man who would have been perfectly at home leaping from a Viking longship, sword in hand, hell-bent on plundering a coastal village or looting a monastery.

When Jaikie presented me, all three saluted distractedly, their attention still fixed on their friend. The lieutenant was introduced to me as Dougal Crombie, a name that struck me as familiar from the world of journalism.

Next was a thick-set, bearded chap wearing the badge of the medical corps. His name was Peter Paterson, though the others addressed him as 'Doc'. Last came the tallest of the three, a slender figure in the uniform and collar of an army chaplain. He was Thomas Yowney, and though his exuberance at the reunion was overlaid by his quiet manner, it was clearly no less than that of his companions.

'Thomas Yowney turned a parson,' laughed Peter. 'Would you credit that, Jaikie? I mind when we were laddies he was dead set on being a pirate.'

'I've found a better treasure than pirate gold,' Yowney responded mildly.

There was a decanter of brandy on a cabinet by the window, which the Die-Hards, from the evidence of the glasses, had already sampled. I poured myself a drink and took a sip, but I was unaware of its quality, so intent was I on the conversation going on between Jaikie and his friends.

'Oh, Jaikie, man, it's a treat to see that wee face of yours again,' Peter enthused.

'Aye, who'd have thought the Die-Hards would be gathered under a roof like this,' said Dougal. 'The rest of the regiment was marching for the coast when these special orders arrived for the three of us to head south.'

'Orders signed by some very impressive people,' Peter added.

'All we had was this location where somebody would bring us further instructions,' said Dougal, 'and who should it turn out to be but the chief scout himself – Jaikie!'

'You might almost think there was somebody behind the scenes pulling the strings,' Thomas suggested meaningfully.

'I think Mr John S. Blenkiron had as much of a hand in it as the Almighty,' said Jaikie.

'Blenkiron?' Dougal made a face. 'That's a right queer name.'

'He's an American,' said Jaikie, 'but he's always been in thick with our own military. He's the one who put this team together.'

'But how did he get wind of the Die-Hards?' Dougal wondered.

'Well, he's been travelling the length of Britain establishing useful contacts,' Jaikie explained, 'and while he was in Scotland he made the acquaintance of Mr Dickson McCunn.'

'I knew it!' Dougal declared, smacking a fist into his palm. 'I knew McCunn would be at the back of it somewhere. The man's that deep, he's capable of anything.'

'Aye, I doubt we'll ever get to the bottom of him,' said Peter, speaking with the authority of a medical man.

'Not without the help of a diving bell,' joked Jaikie.

'So what else has Mr McCunn been up to?' Thomas asked.

'He's in command of his local Home Guard,' Jaikie answered with a grin. 'He's as happy as can be drilling his motley crew of grocers and bank clerks. He marches them up and down the hill, just like the Grand Old Duke, then flings them all into a ditch to practise concealment.'

'I dare say he's applying his sound business principles to the matter of home defence,' said Peter. 'If any Germans ever make it as far as the Canonry, they'll have the devil of a fight on their hands.'

'Aye, old McCunn was never one to go down easy,' Dougal agreed.

From what Archie and Jaikie had told me earlier, I gathered that the almost legendary Dickson McCunn was a retired Glasgow grocer who had taken the Die-Hards under his wing while they were still children. Acting as their protector and mentor, he had raised them out of poverty and paid for their education, so opening up the path that had led them to their present careers. To this day they held him in an esteem bordering on awe.

Two of the original Die-Hards were not present here, by name of Bob and Napoleon. One had long ago emigrated to Canada, the other to Australia, but Jaikie told his friends he had received word that both of their old comrades had found ways to serve the mother country in their adopted lands.

After relating this news, Jaikie directed them towards me. They stood to attention but I waved them back to their seats.

'Relax, gentlemen. It's years since I was last in uniform, so you don't have to treat me like a general.'

'If you don't mind my asking, sir,' Peter ventured, 'what is a general doing in an operation like this?'

'It's not so much because of my battlefield experience,' I replied, 'though I've more than enough of that. It's rather because I have a knack of stumbling into the right place at just the right time, partly by instinct and partly by sheer luck. This mission will need plenty of both.'

'Well, sir, I suppose this is your army,' said Jaikie. 'Dougal here, Lieutenant Crombie, has always been our chief, and we follow him like he was Robert the Bruce.'

'I thought I'd heard of you as somebody high up in the world of journalism, Lieutenant Crombie,' I said.

'Just plain Dougal will do fine,' he said. 'It's true that my boss, Mr Craw of the Craw Press has done all he can to make me indispensable to his business, leaving him the leisure to enjoy the finer things in life. Just to keep him honest, though, I've made a habit of sending myself away on lengthy overseas assignments, forcing him to keep one foot in the business. When this trouble started brewing I appointed myself Chief Military Correspondent.'

He made a self-mocking show of the airs that should be expected of one with so grand a title.

'I told Craw I wouldn't sit behind a desk passing out propaganda. No, I was going to be out there on the front line with the troops. Well, Craw made a few phone calls and next thing I knew I was being put through officer training. He calculated it was a lot safer to make me an officer than to leave me in the ranks where I was liable to stir up a mutiny.'

'Aye, we do sometimes have to hold Dougal back from sticking his head into the lion's mouth,' joked Peter.

'I'm wise enough to follow our trusty scout though,' said Dougal, placing a hand on Jaikie's shoulder. 'Jaikie could find his way blindfolded through a coal mine at midnight.'

'Peter here, as you can see, is our medic,' said Jaikie. 'I expect Mr Blenkiron picked him out in case Mr Roland needs medical attention.'

'If he's been subjected to interrogation, that's more than likely,' I said.

'Though I'm a healer now,' Peterson asserted bullishly, 'I'm still a Die-Hard and you'll not see me shy away from a fight.'

I had no doubt of his fighting spirit, but now I turned to the fourth of the Die-Hards. 'I see we have a chaplain as well. For our spiritual needs?'

'The Reverend Thomas Yowney isn't just here because he can recite half the King James Bible from memory,' said Jaikie.

'No,' said Dougal, 'the fact is, he's the best man you'll find for sheer brains north or south of the border.

There's no spot so tight that he can't think his way out of it.'

Thomas's three friends grinned at each other and chorused, 'Ye'll no' fickle Thomas Yowney!' They finished with a whoop of good-natured laughter that left their companion looking abashed.

'They're exaggerating, of course,' he said diffidently. 'But they mean well.'

In the last war I had commanded thousands of good men and had always taken pride in their courage and loyalty. I could tell even now that this little band from the slums of Glasgow would be among the finest I had ever served with.

I explained to them the outlines of what we were about to undertake and found them eager to tackle the mission. We were discussing transport and equipment when a soldier appeared at the door and summoned me to a private meeting with Captain Leconte.

11

BESIDE THE STILL WATERS

———

When I entered his office Leconte was standing at the window looking out to the north. Without a word he beckoned me to join him and I saw in the distance flames casting a lurid glow upon the cloudy night sky.

'It is a sight, is it not?' he said. 'The Forêt d'Espigny has been set ablaze by German artillery, but already the fire dies away. The fire we face tomorrow will not be so easily quenched, I think.'

'I wish there was some way I could help, but tomorrow we must go to Paris.'

He turned to me and raised a quizzical eyebrow. 'Paris? There will be no defence of Paris. It has been declared an open city.'

'We're going as civilians, and not to fight,' I told him. 'But our mission may be as important as the outcome of any battle.'

'Ah yes, your secret purpose. I don't suppose it matters now if you tell me or not.'

'All I know is that the future course of the war may depend on it.'

'Then let us hope the war will continue at least a little longer, until you achieve your goal.'

I glanced at the map of the château which was now pinned to the wall beside a painting of some shepherds in Arcadia. 'Surely it would be better for you to retreat, join the rest of your army and regroup?'

Leconte frowned. 'To what end? It is no secret our government is resolved on surrender.'

'Then why make this impossible stand?'

He turned back to the window and gazed out over the benighted land.

'Many of my men are from this region. I myself was born only a few miles from here. A man can only abandon so much before he sickens of it. We are forbidden to defend Paris, so we shall make our stand here.'

'But you are so few . . .'

'We have weapons and we are resolved. The rest lies in the hands of the good God.'

He walked over to his desk and picked up a bottle of Tanqueray. 'There are many vintage wines stored here, but instead I chose for you this bottle of gin. You English have a great liking for gin, do you not?'

'Under the right circumstances, yes.'

'What circumstances could be better than this? Two soldiers, each on his way to his own battle, like two riders crossing paths in the night. Surely two such men should share a special drink.'

He poured two glasses and handed one to me.

'When the Germans made their last great assault in nineteen eighteen,' I told him, slowly swirling the drink around the glass, 'I had to hold the line with only the depleted remnant of my regiment. The men fought with a tenacity that was scarcely credible, but if the Germans had realised how weak we were they would have destroyed us. We held on in the hope of reinforcement. What is your hope, Captain?'

'Hope? My hope is that I shall see my wife and

children again. My fear is that it will not be so.'

He tapped a finger against his glass, then he said, 'You have family?'

'My wife is bent on getting back into uniform,' I replied. 'My son is a pilot in the RAF.'

Leconte nodded approvingly. 'They are fine fliers, those men.'

I felt a chill as I recalled Archie's prediction of the next phase of the war. 'They'll need to be.'

He raised his gin in salute and I returned the gesture.

'La Garde meurt,' he toasted, 'mais ne se rend pas.'

We touched glasses and drank.

We breakfasted at dawn on rations provided by our hosts, this being washed down with a glass of wine for each man requisitioned from the château cellars. The Die-Hards had rummaged through the servants' quarters to scrounge up some civilian clothing and were now decked out in an odd assortment of shirts, collars, ties, waistcoats and jackets. Peter had even found a bowler hat which was perched on his head at a rakish angle. Dougal had arranged our transport and we were collecting our gear when Captain Leconte appeared in the doorway of our quarters.

Approaching Thomas, he spoke to him in a confidential tone. 'You are a priest, no? If so, it would be a great favour if you would say a short mass for my men.'

'I am a clergyman, true enough,' said Thomas, 'though not of your persuasion. I can't do you a mass, but I would be happy to lead your men in a prayer.'

'That will suffice,' said Leconte with a brisk nod.

All those who could be spared from keeping watch and the preparation of additional defences were gathered in the huge entrance hall. The Reverend Thomas Yowney addressed them from the marble steps while the rest of us kept to one side.

Since meeting Thomas, I had hardly heard him utter more than a few words. Now, however, when the need for it was so great, he seemed to open up a wellspring of eloquence inside himself. As the Scottish chaplain spoke, the lieutenant repeated his words in French. The repetition of each sentence took on the rhythm of a call and response, passing back and forth like a litany.

'My friends, a time like this brings a man face to face with his religion, and some of you will ask yourselves, *Why must such things be? Why cannot God simply make the world a perfect place of peace?*

'God did make the world a place of peace, but He gave us the power to destroy that peace. If we could not do wrong, we would simply be His puppets and there would be no virtue in doing right. In a world without pain or hardship there would be no courage or compassion. If we had no troubles to face, what need would there be for us to even love one another? And so we choose the good, even when that is the hard choice, even when it costs us dearly.

'And when we have passed through this vale of trouble, will the world be a better and fairer place for all our sufferings? I cannot promise that, for as high as a man climbs, the path is slippery and his weakness drags him down. But I do know this: we all have justice in our hearts. And justice demands that there must be an afterlife, where the hurts of this world are healed and made good, where we will rejoin the dear ones we have lost and sit down to break bread with God Himself.'

As Leconte translated the last sentence, Thomas bowed his head in prayer. At the sight of this, the French soldiers removed their caps and did likewise.

'The Lord is my shepherd,' Thomas began, 'I shall not want. He maketh me to lie down in green pastures; He leadeth me beside the still waters.'

Even without prompting from their commander, the soldiers recognised the ancient psalm and joined in in their own tongue.

'*Il restaure mon âme, Il me conduit dans les sentiers de la justice, à cause de son nom.*'

Familiar with the words from our own childhoods, the Die-Hards and I joined in. All of the voices, English and French, filling the great hall took on a sombre resonance, like the harmony of a choir.

'Yes, though I walk through the valley of the shadow of death, I will fear no evil; for Thou art with me, Thy rod and Thy staff they comfort me.'

'*Tu dresses devant moi une table, en face de mes adversaires; Tu oins d'huile ma tête, et ma coupe déborde.*'

From the far distance came the first boom of artillery, but the centuries-old song of David rolled on without a pause.

'Surely goodness and mercy will follow me all the days of my life and I will dwell in the house of the Lord for ever.'

A final 'Amen' arose from everyone at once and the concluding silence hung upon the air like a blessing. Another crash of artillery sounded from beyond the walls and Leconte gave the order for battle. The soldiers crossed themselves, replaced their caps and began to disperse to their assigned positions.

'I've never been much for churches,' Dougal told Thomas, 'but you lend a manly vigour to your Bible talk that makes it as bracing as a shot of the best malt.'

'Your words were well chosen,' I complimented the chaplain, 'and so was your prayer. I feel quite bad about leaving.'

'And from the sound of those guns outside,' said Jaikie, 'we don't have much time to get clear.'

Briskly we followed Dougal out to a garage that lay adjacent to the west wing of the château. He presented us with our transport, a blue limousine.

'It's a Delage D8,' he said, jumping onto the running board. 'We're travelling in style today, boys. She's fuelled up and ready to go.'

We stowed our gear in the back and Dougal got behind the wheel.

'Could you not find a chauffeur's uniform?' Peter quipped.

The driver grinned. 'Another crack like that, Peter, and you'll be walking to Paris.'

I joined him up front while the other Die-Hards climbed into the rear seats.

The engine spluttered once or twice then purred smoothly as we rolled out onto the driveway. The guards at the gate saluted as we passed by.

'That's a fine bunch of lads back there,' said Dougal. 'I'd half a mind to stick with them, but we've our own fish to fry.'

'I'm sure there's a fight ahead of us, if that's what you want,' said Jaikie.

'I never thought I'd be caught up in another war in France,' I said. 'I expect many brave men will die before it's over.'

'This time we need to be sure there's a better world at the end of it,' said Dougal vehemently. 'There's plenty of us won't stand by and let the politicians and the businessmen help themselves to the peace.'

'You might go in for politics yourself then,' Thomas suggested quietly, 'if you're wanting to remake the world.'

'Ach, I've toyed with the notion,' said Dougal, 'but I'd be no good at it. There's no man alive I won't offend at some point with the fire and vinegar of my views. Talking sweet and oily to win votes would sit ill with me. No, put me at the head of a mob and I'll storm the doors of Parliament, or point me towards the barricade and I'll be the first man to leap on to it. But don't ask me to go from stump to stump telling each man whatever it is he wants to hear. I'd be calling them rogues and wasters and expect them to cheer me for it.'

'Well, if ever the times called for a man of action instead of talk,' said Jaikie, 'this is it.'

'You know,' said Peter, 'you do see some queer sights in wartime. I mind that time we were beating a hasty retreat towards Le Transloy, marching by night to avoid the bombers. There were fires still burning from the day's shelling, and that helped to light the way. At one point our leading section stopped dead and I went to find out what was up. Everybody was listening to a squeaking noise that was coming towards us. After a few moments out of the smoke and darkness came a soldier in a Balmoral, swinging a tin bucket at his side. It was that that was making the noise.

'"Man, where in hell do you think you're going?" I asked him. Says he, showing me his rusty pail, "Ah'm looking for a coo tae mulk." "Well, you'd best turn around," I told him, "because there's nothing behind us but Germans." "Fair enough," says he. "There's another ferm further back. I'll try that."' Around he turns and off he goes, completely unperturbed, like he was taking a stroll down a farm path in Perthshire or Angus!'

There was a short burst of laughter in the car, then we heard the drone of an aircraft passing high overhead. Friend or foe, we could not tell. Behind us, we knew, the armoured might of Germany was advancing in an inexorable tide.

Ahead of us lay Paris – and the secret of the thirty-one kings.

PART TWO
THE CITY OF LIGHT

12

A KNIGHT ERRANT

Even as we entered the outskirts of Paris we perceived the sense of doom hanging over the city. There were few people on the streets. Now and then we glimpsed nervous faces peeking out from behind half closed curtains, as if these lingering citizens were afraid of what they might see passing in the street.

There were very few motor vehicles about and almost no one on foot. Even cyclists were few and far between and none of those had the jaunty air they were accustomed to display as they wove casually through the traffic. Some shops were still open for business, but many had shutters over the window and notices on the door announcing they were closed for the duration of the 'emergency'.

Wending our way past squares and parks we saw trenches that had been dug months before to provide shelter against a bombardment that now would never come. On some of the side streets dispirited civilians were pulling down barricades which had been rendered futile by the surrender of the city. I felt as if we were driving through the aftermath of a battle that had already been lost. It was such a bleak spectacle, I was glad when Dougal broke the silence inside the car.

'Since we're here to find this Roland character, it would help if we knew a bit more about him.'

'Roland is a false name he uses to keep his true

identity safe from the Germans,' I said. 'So we know very little about him.'

'Mr Blenkiron has a hunch as to his true identity,' Jaikie added, 'and if he's correct, then I was acquainted with the man at Cambridge.'

'And that man would be . . . ?' Dougal prompted.

Jaikie shook his head gravely. 'I'm under orders not to speak his name. For one thing, the fewer of us who know, the more secure he is. For another, if Mr Blenkiron's hunch is wrong, then I would be misleading Mr Hannay and the rest of you, sending you off on a false trail while time ticks away.'

His fellow Die-Hards were clearly unhappy with this secrecy, but I came to Jaikie's defence.

'I think you and Blenkiron have reasoned this out correctly. I have some leads of my own to follow, and you, Jaikie, must know the habits of your old college friend.'

He nodded. 'That I do. Knowing what his passions and pastimes are, I can try to pick up his trail from that.'

'What about the rest of us?' enquired Dougal, not entirely pacified.

'You'll establish a command base for us at the Louis Quinze hotel,' I instructed. 'We need to be assured of supplies and transport for a speedy getaway once we've found Roland.'

The habitually silent Thomas spoke up. 'And we had best try to discover what is the safest route out of the city.'

'The Germans are closing in from all sides,' said Peter gruffly, 'but if there is a way out, I'd trust you to find it, Thomas.'

'Let me off here,' I said as we drove down the Boulevard de Clichy. 'I have an errand to run close by.'

Dougal pulled in at the kerb. 'Should we not go with you?'

'A whole gang of us moving around together will be too conspicuous,' I said. 'You go on to the hotel and I'll meet you there.'

Blenkiron had given me the address of a contact of his, the man who had acted as an intermediary for Mr Roland. With the city at least half deserted, I had a notion that enemy agents would be able to act with increasing impunity, and I did not want to tip my hand by having the Die-Hards in my company. Should anything happen to me, they would still be free to carry on with the mission.

Jaikie wished me luck as I climbed out and they drove off down the Rue Fontaine into town. Outside the confines of the car I became even more aware of the taut atmosphere pervading the city. In spite of the diamond bright sky and the fresh summer breeze, the air itself felt heavy with an awful oppression.

On my visits to Paris during the last war, the city had defiantly maintained its gaiety in spite of the battles raging to the north and east. The enemy had been stopped at the gates and the very survival of Paris was a cause for celebration with every new sunlit day.

Now as I walked through Montmartre, even the Sacré-Coeur, in all its lofty beauty, looked lonely and as fragile as an eggshell. The few people I passed in the street avoided my gaze and hunched their shoulders as though weighted down by the imminence of disaster. A line from *The Pilgrim's Progress* ran through my mind, a passage that spoke of 'the powers and terrors of what is yet unseen'.

I passed a closed-up butcher's shop and a bakery that was open for business, though there were only a few loaves and some stale croissants on display. The breeze brought a scent of burning and I saw rising above the rooftops the smoke of several bonfires. I wondered if they were intended as a signal or a warning.

Then, as I rounded the corner I heard the voices of two men, their speech loud and slurred. They had a young woman pressed against a wall and were offering her a swig of wine. Each had an open bottle in his hand and more bottles protruded from their coat pockets. I had an intuition that none of these had been paid for but were looted from an abandoned shop.

When I hailed them they turned their bleary eyes upon me and I guessed that they had begun their day with a breakfast of wine and intended to continue with this diet until the invaders arrived. I saw now that the woman had a pretty, slender face, with bright coral lipstick decorating her generous mouth. Her blonde hair was fashionably done up in curls and she wore a feathered bonnet that matched the colour of her jade green jacket and skirt. She looked uneasy rather than frightened, but I still felt she was in need of assistance.

'My friends, you should not offer wine to my sister,' I informed them in my most affable French.

'Your sister?' one of them bleated in surprise.

'Yes, I have told her so many times not to wander out by herself.' I drew closer. 'But will she listen? No!'

'Your sister?' the other drunkard repeated blankly.

'Yes, she is forever finding ways to make trouble. Why, even a drop of wine turns her into a very she-devil. I once saw her smash a bottle across a man's face because he spilled the merest drop of coffee onto her wrap.'

'You need to take care of her,' the first man advised me in an overly serious tone. They were both backing away and I saw a quirk of amusement on the young woman's lips.

'Ah, Joseph, you never let me have any fun,' she pouted.

'What you call fun, the police call criminal assault,' I informed her severely.

I gently took her by the arm and led her away from the drunks who staggered off in the other direction, making a desultory attempt at the first bars of a popular song.

'So you are my brother?' she said in a friendly voice.

'They might have felt obliged to show that they were not cowed by a husband, who would be viewed as a rival for your admiration.' I removed my hand from her arm. 'Most men have a sister who tries them, however, so that established a bond that removed the need for any confrontation.'

'Thank you for your assistance,' she said. 'I do not think they meant any harm, but . . .'

'If they carry on the way they are, they may cease to be amusing,' I warned. 'This is not a time for a young lady to be out alone.'

'Everyone has their own way of coping with this terrible waiting,' she said. 'For them it is wine, for me it is this.'

She displayed a daintily wrapped box of chocolates which she held in one gloved hand. 'My favourite confectioner is leaving Paris today and I could not face the future without one last box of his most excellent chocolates. May I offer you one?'

'It would be a shame to spoil such beautiful wrapping,' I declined. 'Have you far to get home?'

'My car is just over there,' she said, pointing to a silver Citroën Cabriolet. 'And I promise to go directly home, without any further need for the intervention of a bold English knight. Your accent reveals that much.'

'My name is Cornelius Brand,' I told her, 'and actually I'm from South Africa.' I had instinctively slipped into a false identity, even in the presence of this harmless girl, for I knew I was now on dangerous ground. Even all these years after the last war, the name of Richard Hannay might still set off an alarm in the wrong quarters.

'Really, Mr Brand? You have come a very long way to get caught up in someone else's war.'

'I'm only here on business. I don't intend to do any fighting.'

'Well, you have won your first minor skirmish,' she said, crossing the road to her car. 'Enjoy your time in Paris, Mr Brand, while it is still possible to do so.'

As she drove off I had the sense that there was something familiar about her. I reckoned that she was typical of a certain sort of Parisian woman, a sort I had met years before, who cared nothing about the rise or fall of the Republic, but would risk everything for the sake of a trivial luxury.

I proceeded to the address Blenkiron had given me in the Rue Dancourt. The street appeared deserted with most of the businesses shuttered. From an open window in an upstairs apartment came the sound of a phonograph playing one of Puccini's arias. Other than that and a few distant car engines, all was quiet.

The sign over the shop read *Ambroise Pellerin, Opticien-Lunetier*. The window shutters were down and I felt my hopes sink at the realisation that my contact may already have fled the city, leaving me with no thread to follow. However, when I tried the door it opened easily and a small bell rang as I entered.

The interior was shrouded in gloom but there was something in the air that put me on alert. This immediate intimation of danger kept me from calling out to the proprietor. Instead I silently drew my pistol and advanced cautiously into the shadows. A small light showed through a bead curtain at the back of the shop. When I reached it I stood to one side with a display of spectacle frames at my back. I reached out one hand and slowly opened a gap in the beads.

When there was no reaction I swiftly moved out of hiding and into the room at the rear. A small overhead light illuminated a series of wall charts and a variety of lenses and other paraphernalia of the optician's trade. At the far end of the room was a low desk which I approached cautiously before peering over the top to the floor behind.

Now I knew what had alerted me to the possibility of danger: it was the scent of death. The body was that of a small, bald-headed man in a grey suit. He lay curled up on the floor behind the desk, and from his pallid flesh and the coagulation of the blood I calculated that he must have been here since the day before. The crushed condition of the skull left me in no doubt he had died instantly from one terrible blow. What was left of his features matched the face in a photograph on the wall, which showed him standing proudly before his newly opened establishment in a much happier time. There was no sign of the murder weapon nor any indication that the place had been ransacked for money.

I had already seen evidence that looting was taking place, but surely it was too much of a coincidence that this man had been killed because he walked in on some would-be thief. No, I was quite certain that it was his connection to Blenkiron and the British intelligence service that had signed his death warrant. With the impending arrival of the Wehrmacht, the enemy had grown bold indeed to commit cold-blooded murder here in Paris.

I quickly checked all the doors and cupboards, mainly out of habit, for the assailant was surely long gone. I slid my pistol back into its holster and wondered what to do. In normal times I would report this discovery to the police, but the times were scarcely normal. On the other hand, the Prefecture might be my most logical port of call.

Once outside I walked for a considerable distance before I caught sight of a taxi cruising slowly in search of a customer. I hailed the vehicle and jumped in the back as soon as it stopped, urging the driver to be off with some haste. It was possible the optician's shop was being watched and that I had been tailed.

I had the driver take us randomly around the city and engaged him in conversation so he would not give too much thought as to why I was doing it.

'Business is very slow, it seems.'

'It is almost dead. First, all the rich people left, and now most of the poor have gone too. You are only my second customer today. The first was hauling a large suitcase and wearing three layers of clothes. He asked me to take him to Marseilles. I explained that would make me late for my supper and sent him to find alternate transport.'

'You're not interested in running away?'

The driver shrugged. 'Where to? I know every street, alley and shortcut in Paris. It would take me years to get to know another city so well. So I stay here. The Germans will use taxis when they get here and there will be many of them. When the Germans leave, everyone else will come back and life will go on.'

'You think the Germans will leave then?' I asked.

'Of course. They will steal what they can and go home. Why would they want the headache of trying to run a city as insane as Paris. Me, I like the insanity. But I would not want to be in charge of it,' he added phlegmatically. 'Now, if we have driven around enough to shake off whatever angry husband is pursuing you, where do you want to go?'

'To the Prefecture of Police.'

He nodded. 'You might as well,' he said. 'Go and confess now to whatever crimes you have committed. By morning they will be bagatelles compared to what is coming.'

13

THE LAST GUARDIANS

We crossed the Pont Notre-Dame to the Île de la Cité and here the driver let me out in the main square in front of the Prefecture of Police. I gave him a large enough tip to put a smile on his face even in this troubled time. As he drove off I hoped it would be of some small help to him through what lay ahead. I gazed across the square at the face of the great Gothic cathedral of Notre-Dame de Paris, with its double doors, its solid, soaring towers and its array of threatening gargoyles perched along the roof. A flight of doves glided between the towers then arced upwards into the sky where I lost them against the brightness of the sun.

For a moment the cathedral took on in my eyes the appearance of a massive rock rising out of a stormy sea, unmoved and unmarked by the crashing waves of war and revolution. Somehow, through all the turmoil, civilisation survived and men learned again to live in peace, turning their energies to better things than killing each other by the thousand.

The thought came to me that, down the centuries, hundreds of others had stood on this spot before me, gazing at the mighty facade, and felt the same realisation wash over them. In ages to come others would stand here again and see eternity itself raised up before them in the ancient stonework.

On a normal day there would be swarms of sightseers here, but today only a few cyclists rolled past the worshippers who were filing despondently into the cathedral. From inside I could hear the faint murmur of Mass and wondered if, against all hope, the faithful were still praying for peace.

I turned away from the mercy of God towards the justice of man. The grey walls of the Prefecture loomed over me, their many windows staring out across the city like the empty eyes of a blind man. Passing through the arched entrance, I sought out the reception area.

It was unexpectedly quiet inside and only a single junior officer sat at the desk. I gave him my name and showed my identification, then asked to be shown to whoever was in charge. Silently I wondered if there was any such person in what was becoming a city of ghosts. He rose and straightened his tunic, then led me up a flight of echoing stairs to the next floor. Ushering me into the Prefect's office, he announced me to his superior and left.

There were two men here: one a short fellow in a smart police uniform, the other a burly civilian smoking a pipe. 'I am the Prefect of Police, Paul Rogeron,' said the officer. He cut a dapper figure in his immaculate blue uniform, the buttons freshly polished as if he expected to review a parade before the day was out. 'In these dangerous times I must ask for some confirmation of your identity.'

As the prefect examined my papers I cast an eye around the room. A large map of the city was flanked by various certificates charting the prefect's ascent up the ranks to his present lofty position. On his desk a photograph of a pretty woman and three children presented an island of domestic simplicity amid a sea of folders and documents.

Rogeron presented my identification to the other man who waved it away and offered me his hand.

'Glad to meet you, Mr Hannay. I'm William Bullitt, the American ambassador.'

He grinned as we shook hands. He was a broad-shouldered man in a rumpled white suit, whose loosened tie and tousled hair suggested that he had spent the past twenty-four hours hard at work. He was smoking a briarwood pipe filled with tarry tobacco. I had the impression that this was his primary source of fuel rather than the coffee and pastries laid out on the desk.

'Mr Bullitt and I comprise what must pass as the government of Paris,' said Rogeron. 'Since our elected officials fled we are left with all their responsibilities.'

'You can think of us as two bewildered mayors,' joked Bullitt. 'Though pretty soon I expect those duties will be taken out of our hands.'

'So many requests,' the prefect sighed, shuffling the documents on his desk, 'so many questions. Should our flags be displayed defiantly or flown at half mast or removed completely? Should the gendarmerie continue in their duties tomorrow or hand all authority over to the occupying force? Should munitions and other supplies be destroyed or left as plunder for the enemy?'

Bullitt thrust a hand into his pocket and jingled some coins. 'I'm still trying to figure out which foreign nationals will be safe here once the Germans move in. For a while the city was crowded with Czechs, Poles, Austrians, Norwegians and so on, but now the population's dropped to a fraction of what it was.'

'Those who are left still require guidance and security,' said Rogeron.

'But those are our troubles, Mr Hannay,' said Bullitt ruefully. 'What brings you here? I don't imagine you're looking for a night out at the Moulin Rouge.'

'I'm here because of a countryman of yours, Mr Bullitt,' I told him, 'John S. Blenkiron.'

'Johnny!' the American exclaimed with a laugh. 'I thought that old bandit had gone to ground. Where's he hanging his hat these days?'

'In all sorts of places, though it was in London I met with him.'

Time was pressing too hard on us for any sort of evasion, so I explained my mission to them as briefly as I could and recounted my discovery of Pellerin's body.

'You're sure it wasn't just some opportunist robber who killed that guy?' said Bullitt, pausing to refill his pipe.

'Very sure,' I replied. 'If we can track down his killer, that could put me on the trail of Roland and his captors.'

'I have very few men left to me,' said Rogeron, spreading his hands apologetically, 'and they are much occupied in keeping any possible looting at bay.'

'What about another tack?' I suggested. 'It's a good guess that Roland has fallen into the hands of a German agent code-named Klingsor.'

'I have heard that name once or twice,' said the prefect.

'Me too,' said Bullitt, 'but I don't know anybody who's ever seen him. It's like he's some kind of phantom.'

'To be perfectly frank with you, Monsieur Hannay,' said Rogeron, 'I'm not sure he exists at all.'

'What have you heard about him?' I pressed, desperate for any information whatsoever.

'Only that he has been here for some considerable time.' He shrugged. 'Bear in mind that Paris has been a refuge for exiles for centuries: Bolsheviks, White Russians, impoverished aristocrats, and political dissidents of every stripe. It is not difficult for a new face to pass unnoticed.'

I clenched my fists in frustration. 'Can you not spare some men to investigate, to round up some suspected enemy agents?'

Rogeron shook his head regretfully. 'Half my men have taken their families and fled. The others have their hands full keeping order and guarding the abandoned homes of the rich and powerful. That is not my own priority but those are the orders left for me.'

'But in a matter this vital . . .'

Bullitt raised a hand to quieten me and let out a puff of smoke. 'Hitler could be taking a stroll down the street right outside, Mr Hannay, and I doubt if we could find enough men to arrest him.'

I made a further appeal to the Frenchman. 'But your own intelligence services must have a file on this Klingsor. That would be something.'

Rogeron beckoned me to the window and gestured at the sky.

'Do you see the smoke rising over the city?'

'Yes, I wondered about that.'

'The clerks left behind by our fleeing rulers are busy burning all government documents. This they were ordered to do to keep them out of German hands. Any information concerning espionage activity in Paris is now flame and ash.'

'What about your own police files?' I suggested. 'Surely you haven't burned them too.'

Rogeron gestured towards the river. 'No, they have been loaded onto a pair of barges and are making their way down the Seine beyond the grasp of the Gestapo.'

'And in case the Germans do catch up with them,' added Bullitt, 'both are packed with explosives and will be blown to smithereens.'

'As well as information on criminals,' said Rogeron, 'there are also files on political dissidents and other radicals. I would not have them identified to our new masters.'

I felt my heart sink. If these two men, who were all that remained of the French government, could not help me, then my cause might well be lost. In the square below I saw Parisians continuing to file into Notre-Dame.

Following my eyes, Rogeron said, 'They seek sanctuary, such as was granted in olden times. Those gargoyles on the roof were placed there to scare away devils.'

Bullitt bit on his pipe and grunted. 'They'll have their work cut out for them tomorrow.'

'Is there nothing you can offer me,' I groaned, 'some other source of information?' In my ears my own voice sounded almost like an appeal for divine intervention.

Bullitt removed his pipe from his mouth and gazed into the bowl, as though there were some omen to be found in the burnt embers of tobacco.

'There is someone who may be able to help,' he said. 'Her name is Beata van Diemen, a Dutchwoman resident in Paris these past two years.'

'A Dutchwoman? What is she doing here?'

'Ostensibly she is a patron of the arts, a dealer in antiques, and a leading socialite. But behind the scenes she's been instrumental in smuggling people out of Germany and getting them to safety.'

'I have heard the name,' said the prefect, 'but I do not believe I have ever met the lady.'

Bullitt gave a dry chuckle. 'I expect the reason she hasn't been cosying up to you, Prefect, is that some of her activities don't exactly fall on your side of the law.'

The policeman raised an enquiring eyebrow.

'Don't get me wrong – she's no crook. But in order to smuggle dissidents of one sort or another out of Germany and get them to safety, she has to bend the more stubborn points of the law. That can necessitate a certain amount of bribery, forgery and other doubtful practices.'

Rogeron conceded the point with a shrug. 'I suppose such transgressions are of little matter now. But she is about to fall under a much heavier brand of justice than any I have ever administered, one which forgives nothing.'

'Anyway,' Bullitt continued, 'because of the many contacts she's built up on every level of society, she's privy to all kinds of information that never makes its way into the papers. If anyone can snag a lead on your missing friend, Hannay, she's the one.'

I leapt at the chance, my heart quickening at this sudden renewal of hope. 'How can I meet her?'

'Well, you can't just charge in, asking a lot of questions. She's wary of such intrusions, as you'd expect.'

'I hardly have the time to wait for a formal introduction,' I pointed out.

'Don't worry,' said Bullitt, reaching into his pocket. 'I have an in for you. She's throwing a party at her house tonight.'

'A curious time for frivolities,' Rogeron noted with a frown.

'Be that as it may,' said Bullitt, 'I have an invite. As you can imagine, I have a lot of pressing business that keeps me from socialising, but there's no reason you can't go in my place.'

He handed me a gilded card bearing an address and an invitation to join *une soirée très exceptionelle*. 'Who on earth would want to be at a party on the eve of anything so dreadful?' I wondered.

'Anyone who has chosen not to flee either welcomes what is coming or seeks a distraction from the horror of it,' Rogeron suggested.

'And since we can bet Klingsor will stick around for sure,' said Bullitt, 'there's a better than even chance he'll be there to toast the coming victory.'

The possibility that the German agent himself might attend clinched the matter for me. I slipped the card into my pocket and thanked the ambassador for his help.

'Don't mention it,' he said. 'I've never been one for parties. I prefer a few hands of poker or a ball game. But you be sure to have a good time.'

I headed for the exit but stopped in the doorway to

look back at the two befuddled mayors, the last guardians of Paris.

'In case we don't meet again, gentlemen, I wish you both the very best of luck.'

'Paris will endure, Mr Hannay,' said Rogeron, though his confidence was tinged with melancholy. 'Whether by guile, prayer or blood, Paris will endure.'

At the Louis Quinze hotel the Die-Hards had booked a suite of rooms on the third floor. Here I found Peter and Thomas, who had ordered a pot of tea and a plate of sandwiches. They informed me that Jaikie was scouting out any possible haunts of the old college acquaintance he had spoken of before. Dougal had accompanied him, declaring that 'somebody has to look out for the lad'.

The chaplain had spread a large map of Paris over the bed. It was dotted with salt cellars, sugar cubes and other objects, which he was moving carefully from place to place while making ruminatory noises in his throat.

'He's working out the most likely route the Germans will take when they come rolling into town,' Peter explained, munching on a baguette filled with ham and Dijon mustard. 'According to the gossip around here, they're expected first thing in the morning.'

'They'll make a triumphal entry down one of the main boulevards,' said Thomas, mostly to himself, 'set up a command base in the centre, and from there spread out to occupy major junctions and government buildings. This will give us an hour. Perhaps more if we're lucky.'

After a bite to eat I took a quick bath and smartened myself up. I explained to my companions what I was up to and gave them Beata van Diemen's address.

'It's an awfy queer time for a party,' Peter grumbled.

'I'm hoping that Klingsor will be there to celebrate his victory,' I said.

'Are you going unarmed?' Peter asked with a frown, noting that I had left my pistol and holster on the table.

'I don't want to arouse any sort of suspicion,' I explained. 'If I'm spotted with a gun, that might put my quarry to flight.'

'Supposing he's there at all,' put in Thomas, looking up from his map.

'It's a long shot,' I agreed, 'but there's also the chance that this woman with her contacts may be able to set me on the right track. I'll try to get back in time to find out if Jaikie's come up with anything.'

'One of you had better strike it lucky pretty soon,' said Peter. 'In a few hours we'll be playing hide and go keek with the Jerries.'

I had the hotel summon a taxi for the Rue Vaneau where the party was taking place. I was headed straight into the lion's den with no idea which of my fellow guests was the lion.

14

THE CONJURER

—

The cab carried me through the quiet twilit streets until we arrived at the Rue Vaneau in the fashionable seventh arrondissement. Stepping out, I saw against the deep red of the western sky a single, solitary light flashing from the summit of the Eiffel Tower – a distress signal that no one would answer.

Beata van Diemen's house was separated from the street by a white wall. The servant at the door gave my invitation a cursory glance and waved me into the courtyard garden. Here a girl in ballet costume was performing an unsteady pas de deux beneath the lantern-lit branches of an elm tree. Seated on a bench, a sleepy, unshaven fellow was strumming his guitar in accompaniment to her efforts. Beside a bed of japonica a couple in dishevelled evening wear lay on the grass staring wanly up at the distant uncaring stars while humming a childhood nursery song.

The building was of cream stone with tall rectangular windows from which light spilled onto the pathway below. I climbed the steps to the front door and walked in on one of the most extraordinary scenes I have ever encountered.

Swing music played on a phonograph but Benny Goodman's clarinet was almost drowned out by the chatter and laughter of the many guests who filled the spacious hallway. A dozen couples danced across a floor of Italian marble, some in evening wear, others in fancy dress. There were harlequins, musketeers and clowns, while a number of the more avant-garde women were dressed defiantly in Palazzo pants and striped tops. They gesticulated languidly with their Russian cigarettes while arguing about abstract art. Overhead a trio of chandeliers gleamed brilliantly, sparking flashes of light from the huge mirrors that lined the gold-painted walls.

A waiter immediately presented me with a glass of Champagne which I sipped distractedly as I ascended a wide stairway carpeted in rich burgundy. The upper floor consisted of a series of interconnecting salons each of which was fully supplied with hors d'oeuvres, more Champagne, and a brittle sense of desperate gaiety. Incongruous paintings from the Low Countries hung on the walls and the practical, plainly dressed Dutch householders glowered disapprovingly at the antics of the guests.

After the Champagne I restricted myself to soda water so as to be fully alert. I had a suspicion that Klingsor would also be keeping a sober, watchful eye on those around him. An instinct I had learned to trust many years ago told me he was certainly here, like a beast of prey lurking in the foliage of a tropical jungle.

To anyone who bothered to ask, I was Cornelius Brand, a South African mining engineer returning from a visit to the Loire coal fields. Fortunately nobody took much note of me, for I must have cut a very dull figure in the midst of such exotic company. When I enquired after our hostess I was informed that she had yet to make an appearance.

In the next room unashamed nudes painted by some of Rubens' less talented imitators capered through sunlit forests, outdoing in innocent gaiety the intense self-indulgence of this party. In one corner a languid youth was regaling his companions with the news that existence had no meaning. In another was a card table where a party of overly rouged women were squealing excitedly over a game of bouillotte.

The adjacent room was hung with French tapestries and dominated by a bronze copy of the Winged Victory. Here, a tall angular man with a golden beard was making coins pass invisibly from one clenched fist to another. He greeted the applause of his inebriated audience with a broad grin then proceeded to draw a string of coloured kerchiefs from the mouth of an astonished woman.

Turning away from his feats of conjuring, I spotted a familiar face coming towards me through the revellers. It was the young lady I had encountered in Montmartre this morning, now dressed in canary-coloured satin beaded with pearls and with a spray of gauze and feathers perched above her brow like a butterfly. Against this background of boredom and excess, she seemed younger than ever, in spite of her make-up and elegant evening wear. She had the look of a girl who has mischievously slipped into her mother's party gown.

'Well,' I declared, 'this is an unexpected pleasure.'

'Surely not unexpected, Mr Brand,' she responded with a smile. 'This is my house after all.'

'Your house? You mean . . .'

'Yes, I am Beata van Diemen.'

'Pardon my surprise – I expected someone older.'

'Grey-haired and serious, you mean. I am so sorry to disappoint you.'

'No disappointment at all. Quite the contrary.'

She offered me her hand, which I took and kissed, feeling as though I were being granted an audience with royalty. As I straightened up I noticed pinned to her breast an antique lacquered brooch decorated with the figure of a winged horse.

'I hope you won't think me rude,' she said as our eyes met again, 'but I don't recall inviting you.'

'Ambassador Bullitt sends his regrets. He's unable to attend, and sent me along in his place.' I cast an appraising glance about the room. 'This is quite the party.'

'Yes, it's all rather ghastly, isn't it?' said Beata with an impish gleam in her eye. 'I can't imagine that you feel very at home here. Which means you have some reason other than entertainment for attending.'

Discreetly she drew me into an alcove where, by some miracle of acoustic science, we were buffered against the worst of the party noise.

'Really, you mustn't judge them too harshly,' she said of her guests. 'This is like the final party on a sinking ship. Tomorrow we all drown – or we learn to swim.'

Though I had come here to seek her help, I was still wary of revealing too much to this elegant young woman. 'So what is it that's keeping you here? You're obviously wealthy enough to escape to some far-off place.'

'You mean like Portugal? Or America even? No, Mr Brand, I fled my own country to escape the horror I foresaw' – she fingered the brooch with its winged horse, as though it symbolised her own flight – 'but I am done with running. I will make my stand here, whatever comes of it.'

'You are a very brave woman.'

'No, I am a frightful coward. My mind is filled with fearful imaginings, but I will not give in to them. I learned this lesson long ago. When I was a child of five, Mr Brand, I had an older friend named Elisa who used to frighten me with awful stories about how goblins would break into my room at night to carry me off and how the strange old man down the street had a long sharp knife he kept to chop up any children who walked too close to his house.'

'She doesn't sound like much of a friend,' I commented.

'Children can be cruel when all they think they are doing is teasing,' said Beata. 'Anyway, she used to frighten me terribly but eventually I dared the goblins to come and they did not. And I walked right up to that old man's door and nothing happened. I overcame my fears. But recently I allowed myself to become a frightened child again. I fled my country to escape the scary man I was afraid was going to come for me. But he is coming here anyway. So it is no use being afraid. I will stand my ground and do what I can.'

'I'm afraid I don't have any childhood stories to explain why I'm here.'

'No, but I'm sure there is a very good reason.'

'To be honest, the matter is a delicate one.'

'Mr Brand, in the morning there will be tanks rolling down that street outside. There is hardly time for delicacy.'

She was right, and I was all too aware of how closely time was pressing on me. 'I need to find a certain man. He's an agent of the German government.'

'If you wait a few hours, you can have your pick of those.'

'I believe he is here now – in this house.'

Beata glanced across the room as she took a sip from her drink. 'I've invited all sorts of people, many on only the briefest acquaintance, and many of them have brought friends I've never seen before. I'm afraid I couldn't vouch for any of them.'

'But I've been told that you are in the business of helping people escape from such men. You have confidential information, contacts.'

She paused in mid-drink, fixing her eye keenly upon me. I understood that in a life such as hers she had to be wary, even of wandering knights.

'Even if that were so,' she began slowly, 'is there nothing more that you can tell me about this man you are so eager to meet?'

'Only that he is referred to by the name Klingsor.'

'Klingsor? I take it then that he is an admirer of Wagner.'

'I should think that's certainly true.'

Beata set her glass aside and her pale blue eyes grew serious. 'You will appreciate that in my line of work, I do my best to avoid contact with agents of Nazi Germany. And yet you have reason to believe he is here.'

'It's more a hunch than any sort of logic. Tomorrow will be his day of triumph. Where else could he safely celebrate out in the open.' I gave her a few seconds to digest this then asked, 'Can you help?'

'Look, I will talk to some people, perhaps make a phone call or two. In the meantime I'll introduce you to the Swiss ambassador. His neutrality makes him a lure for all manner of gossip and he knows absolutely everybody. To be frank he's a bit of a bore, but I promise to get back to you with something.'

She took me by the arm and guided me to where a portly man in spectacles was selecting samples from a platter of truffles.

'Rudi,' she said, 'this is Mr Cornelius Brand from South Africa. He's quite at sea here and you would be doing me an enormous favour if you could help him make a few new friends.'

The ambassador's mouth was quite full so he could only nod in acknowledgement. When Beata had glided away he scrutinised me like I was seeking the hand of his daughter.

'Come with me, Mr Brand,' he said in a surprisingly high-pitched voice. 'Let's see if we can find some fascinating company for you.'

To begin with he introduced me to merchants of one kind or another who would not leave their successful businesses behind and whose only fear was that the current crisis would lead to a drop in the markets. Next I made the acquaintance of several minor French functionaries who seemed oddly proud that they would be handing over to their new masters an admirably efficient bureaucracy.

When my guide felt he had done his duty by me, he squeezed onto a divan with an equally plump lady to share a plate of éclairs, leaving me to my own devices.

However, as I wandered about the room, I noticed that from time to time this Rudi was casting veiled glances in my direction. Did he still feel a sense of the responsibility laid upon him by our hostess, I wondered, or did those languid eyes belong to someone far more dangerous than a mere gourmand?

As the food and drink made the company more and more garrulous, I was easy prey for anyone who felt in need of a new friend or of a fresh ear to talk into. I was treated to the profound political insights of actors, painters and – worst of all – poets. For what felt like an eternity a belligerent pacifist bombarded me with the unassailable truth that this whole catastrophe was the fault of his own French government and their treacherous English allies.

I disengaged myself with as much grace as I could muster and, following the sound of a piano, took refuge in the next room. Here, a highly-strung woman with tear-filled eyes was working hard at turning Debussy's 'Clair de Lune' into a dirge.

I was beginning to feel a similar sense of despair. I still had no clue as to which of these guests was Klingsor and I was wondering when Beata van Diemen would ever return. Then I chided myself for my poor attitude. I had not come through so much simply to give up. No, I had to think my way through this.

I had encountered enemy agents before, chief among them the Kaiser's most brilliant spy, von Schwabing. He was a master of hiding himself in plain sight, taking on a false identity so impenetrable that even when I was certain my foe sat before me, I still had trouble believing that this affable, tennis-playing Englishman could be my primary foe.

That was his greatest skill and his greatest satisfaction, to hide in the open with the light shining fully upon him. What if Klingsor were doing the same thing? Rather than sitting in some dark corner talking in whispers, would he not take a special pleasure in showing off in front of the whole party?

At once my thoughts turned to the amateur conjurer whose performance I had paused to watch earlier this evening. Could it be that simple? Was Klingsor so arrogant that he would adopt the name of a wizard from Wagner's *Parsifal* and was now entertaining an unsuspecting audience with his sleight of hand?

I moved swiftly through the bustling interconnected salons until I found him. He was relaxing with a cigarette and sipping a martini, but at the high-spirited urging of his fellow guests, he stood up to an appreciative burst of applause. He plucked a deck of cards from his pocket and immediately began to demonstrate his dexterity by fanning them and then making individual cards vanish, only for them to reappear in the pocket of some astonished onlooker.

'Who is that extraordinary gentleman?' I asked a nearby lady once she had stopped applauding.

'Leo O'Riordan,' she replied. 'I believe he is a journalist for the *Irish Times*. Isn't he marvellous?'

'Yes, he's very skilled.'

I observed closely as O'Riordan made handfuls of cards vanish into thin air. His concealment of his true identity was just as brilliant, and I resolved to force the issue with him at the first opportunity. Fluent as I was in German, I was sure I could convince him that I had arrived with urgent news from Berlin. Once I had him alone I would find the means to unmask him. I was pondering my strategy when I felt a sudden presence at my elbow.

I turned to see Beata van Diemen standing there. Even though she was the glamorous hostess of the evening, she seemed to have passed unnoticed across the room, as if cloaked in a mist of invisibility from an old fairy tale. I reflected that as she was much occupied in helping fugitives escape from enemy territory, she must have become well practised at moving unseen through a crowd.

'Mr Brand,' she said in a low, urgent whisper, 'I think I may be able to help you after all. We must speak privately.'

I directed her attention to the golden-bearded Irishman. 'I'm almost sure that man with the cards is the one I'm looking for.'

A vexed frown creased the smoothness of her brow. 'You must not confront him now,' she insisted. 'To do so would be disastrous. Come, we must talk where prying ears cannot reach.'

She set off across the room without further instruction, trusting me to understand that I was to follow. She drew a key from her purse to unlock a small cream-coloured door which led to a narrow stairway. Locking up behind us, she led me to an upper floor where we entered a brightly lit study.

She poured us each a glass of brandy. As soon as she

handed me mine she threw hers back in one swallow and set the glass aside.

'Go ahead,' she urged me with a sad smile. 'You will need a drink when you hear what I have to tell you.'

Foolish as it was, I had the strange sense that she would not divulge her information unless I took my brandy as she had done. I knocked it back in a single gulp, feeling the warmth of it slip down my throat, and met her cool gaze.

'There,' she said approvingly. 'You had best sit down now.'

'Is what you have learned really so shocking?' I asked.

'It is,' she affirmed. 'More so than you could ever have guessed.'

She walked around the room, lightly touching a finger to the various pieces of ornamental porcelain. She appeared lost in thought, reflecting on the gravity of our situation.

I was actually feeling a little woozy, and so was happy to oblige her by sitting down on a chintz chair. The room seemed suddenly very warm and I had to fight back a wave of nausea. With an effort I fixed my shaky vision upon her as she ceased her wandering and came towards me.

'Tell me,' I said, 'what have you learned about Klingsor?' My words sounded strangely slow and slurred to my ears.

Beata loomed over me, appearing much taller than before, as if her slight frame were elongating before my eyes.

'I am afraid he has unmasked you first, Mr Hannay.' Her voice echoed as though we were in the centre of some vast marble tomb.

'Hannay?' My thoughts were sluggish, but I knew something was amiss. 'My name is . . . Brand . . . Cornelius Brand.'

'So you told me – Cornelius Brand, the South African mining engineer,' she retorted mockingly. 'But in fact you are Sir Richard Hannay, soldier, war hero – and *spy*.'

There was an acidic bite to the last word that cut through the haze that was enveloping me. I tried to speak, but my tongue was numb.

'Poison!' I choked at last, realising too late just what a gullible fool I had been.

All around me the room was dissolving, like a painting in oils melting under an extreme heat. Objects were losing their boundaries, the colours spilling into each other in a dizzying swirl that threw me into a spasm of vertigo.

Beata leaned closer, but all I could see of her face were her small white teeth exposed in a smile as frigid as an Arctic gale.

'Did you think I would not see through your boyish deceit, Mr Hannay – I, who for years have studied every dossier on you? You and Mr John Scantlebury Blenkiron. And of course your dear friend Sandy Arbuthnot, Lord Clanroyden.'

There was no mirth in her words now, only a terrible, savage hatred. And, as the fatal darkness sucked me down, I knew precisely who she was.

15

THE BLIGHTED SPIRIT

———

Out of the darkness came a swirl of dust from which emerged a small rocky hill in the centre of a valley. A hollow in the summit created a natural fort defended by three men with half a dozen armed followers. Obscured by the haze, they looked like the ghostly remnant of an abandoned garrison while the sighing of the wind was like a lament for all that would be lost here.

A blonde woman climbed the rugged slope, her pale blue eyes ablaze with a passion somewhere between love and vengeance. She carried a flag of peace, though everything in her manner spoke of war. The three soldiers watched her approach with something like awe in their faces and one of them appeared on the brink of fainting.

When she reached the crude fort the woman spoke in a voice charged with the bitterness of betrayal and the persisting hope of glory. The man she addressed, the one with haunted eyes, listened as though entranced by a siren's song. The conflict tearing at his heart was evident in his tortured features as he finally rejected her offer in a voice as dry as sand.

Her brilliant eyes flashed in fury and she laid a final curse upon him before starting back towards her own lines. It was then that the shells began to fall and a cry of anguish burst from the man's lips.

That cry echoed in my ears as I struggled back to consciousness. I felt as though I were sunk in a devouring marsh and it was taking all my strength to fight my way up to the open air. When I cracked open my eyes they were stabbed by the harsh glare of an unshaded light bulb hanging overhead. At my first attempt to move I discovered I was bound hand and foot to a stout wooden chair with bonds that were more than tight enough to hold me in my weakened state.

I felt sick to my stomach and my head lolled drunkenly to one side. Slowly my vision cleared to the point where I could absorb my surroundings. The walls were white-washed brick, the floor uncarpeted boards, and the furnishings limited to a couple of straight-backed chairs and a small round table. I guessed I was in the cellar of Beata van Diemen's house, though this room was a bare contrast to the elegant chambers above. I recalled the drink, the sudden crippling sickness, and my own stupidity at allowing myself to be so easily drugged.

There was only one door that I could see and it was firmly shut. Standing in front of it, still incongruously dressed in her party finery, Beata van Diemen was touching a silver lighter to a cigarette. When she noticed me stirring she took in a long draw of smoke and glanced at her jewelled wristwatch. Exhaling slowly, she viewed me through the smoke as though I were a newly acquired objet d'art.

'You recover quickly,' she said. 'It's only been a few hours.'

There was a bitter taste in my mouth and I supposed I must have retched before losing consciousness. Licking my dry lips, I struggled to find my voice. 'I hope I haven't missed the party.'

I sounded like a feeble child at the end of a coughing fit.

A half-smile twisted one corner of her painted mouth. 'Good. You can still make light of the situation. The guests are gone now, returned home to tremble in their beds as they wait for their conquerors to come marching down the street. That will be a sight to see, will it not?'

'Your people do have a flair for pageantry.' I paused to work up some moisture in my mouth. My tongue felt like a dry dish rag, but I was determined not to meet her gloating with silence. 'A bit too theatrical for my taste. I'd sooner watch the Life Guards on parade.'

She was keeping her distance, viewing me from afar as she smoked. As I focused on her scornful eyes, I could not deny that she still looked beautiful, even though I now knew her for what she was. It was a savage beauty I had encountered only once before.

I had not followed my own chain of reasoning to its logical conclusion. If Klingsor was hiding in plain sight, taking sly satisfaction from being the centre of attention, there was no one more obvious than the hostess of the party. She, after all, had arranged these revels, and it was clear now that she was celebrating her own victory.

Noting the intensity of my gaze, she said, 'So, Mr Hannay, have you recognised me at last as the very adversary you were seeking?'

'I should have done so earlier,' I admitted. 'From the very first I was aware of something familiar.'

'Really? Is the resemblance so strong?'

'Enough to have warned me that you are Hilda von Einem's daughter.' Even as I spoke the words, the enormity of it shook me to the core. So many years ago, and those fateful events still had me ensnared.

Hilda von Einem was the most brilliant of the Kaiser's agents and she had guided events in the east to the brink of a Mohammedan uprising that would have set the whole region aflame. My friend Sandy Clanroyden, in the guise of a fanatical mystic, had infiltrated her inner circle so completely that he became the linchpin of her scheme. When he turned against her the whole magnificent enterprise came crashing down into the dust and that astonishing woman was killed in an artillery bombardment mere moments after making a final effort to regain Sandy's allegiance.

Beata was silent, letting the ash fall from her cigarette as though her thoughts had also drifted back to another time and place.

'I think it was the eyes,' I said, recalling how unafraid she had been of the two drunken oafs. 'Yes, you definitely have her eyes.'

She drew closer and stared daggers at me. 'If that is true, then you must see the hate in them.'

Her embittered gaze was as bleak as the bare light above. I lowered my head and fought my way through the lingering fog that still engulfed my thoughts. After a few seconds I forced myself to look up. 'Hate is a shabby, desiccated thing, you know. Once it takes root it blights the spirit and nothing else can grow.'

She gave a short, hard laugh. 'Are you trying to dispense wisdom? It comes very hollow from the lips of one who has been so easily duped.'

She paced around me, disappearing from view behind my back.

Her bitter voice continued. 'When we met by chance in Montmartre you imagined me a damsel in distress and you have been unable to shake off that impression. That very English sense of chivalry has proved your undoing. I could not have devised a more perfect blind.'

An awful realisation dawned on me that all along she had been in complete control of my actions. 'You knew me even then? Right from that first moment?'

She was still out of sight, lending her voice the uncanny quality of a disembodied presence. 'I was familiar with your appearance from some old photographs in our files, but the resemblance was not conclusive. It was the name Cornelius Brand that gave you away. You really are overly fond of that alias.'

'I find it safer to use a name I can answer to instinctively. I'm happy to admit that when it comes to deceit, you have me beaten. You've tricked a lot of people into thinking that you're a saviour of those fleeing the very regime you serve.'

Beata came into view, her high heels clicking on the bare wooden floor. While her back was to me I tugged at my bonds, but the knots had been expertly tied.

'Oh, I have genuinely helped many of them escape,' she said, turning to face me, 'but only those of little importance. About one in ten is someone we do not wish to go free, and they do not escape. Some flaw in their false papers or other piece of bad luck guarantees their return to the homeland to face justice. And I remain unsuspected, of course, lamenting each of those few failures.'

I knew what was involved in creating and maintaining such a perfect and false persona. 'I suppose your charming story of childhood courage was just that – a story.'

'No, Mr Hannay, it was true, but incomplete, which is the secret of any effective falsehood. You see, the day after I stood upon the doorstep of the old man's house I decided to take my revenge on Elisa for frightening me so. I waited in ambush for her to come riding her bicycle by the canal, as she did every day. She suspected nothing when I jumped out and pushed her into the water.'

There was an almost childlike glee in Beata's voice as she remembered, which rendered her tale even more horrific.

'She screamed, and she heard me laugh as she splashed into the cold, muddy water. She struggled in a blind panic, desperate to disentangle herself from her bicycle. She came within a hair's breadth of drowning and I have never forgotten the look of craven terror on her face as she crawled onto the bank. I knew then what it was to master one's fears and turn them against others.'

She stubbed out her cigarette and faced me squarely. 'I believe it was even then that I began planning my revenge upon you and your two noble friends.'

Appalled though I was, I could not help but feel a pang of remorse for this girl who had grown up devoid of kindness or compassion so that now she stood before me like a twisted shadow of her mother's greatness.

'You must have had something better than that in your life,' I whispered, 'a family, a father . . .'

'I had neither,' Beata snapped, 'only the tales that

were told me of my mother's heroic struggle – and of her betrayal.'

'We were all of us doing our duty,' I said. I sounded like a defendant pleading in court, though I had no doubt sentence had already been passed. 'She did not die by our hand and we buried her with honour.'

'I damn your honour!' spat the girl. 'And I damn you too. All three of you. I had a hunt planned, Hannay, a year from now when England will have fallen. I was going to track you all down like beasts and relish your slow, painful deaths. I did not expect you to come running to me.' She paused to flick away a small piece of ash from her sleeve. 'I suppose it was the thirty-one kings that flushed you out.'

I did my best to show no flicker of recognition at the phrase. 'I've no idea what you're talking about.'

Beata eyed me scornfully. 'Oh, come now, why else would you be seeking out Klingsor at this late stage of the game? You wanted to find the man named Roland.'

She leaned towards me, smiling as she ran a finger around the winged horse on her brooch, using this symbol of freedom to mock my helplessness.

My head was clearing now and my thoughts began to move swiftly. There was no use denying my purpose and perhaps there was a slim chance of gaining some information even now.

'I suppose you're holding him prisoner here just like me,' I said in a voice that was deliberately hopeless.

'Here? In my own home?' The notion seemed to amuse her. 'No, I would not keep so valuable an item here. Rest assured he is stored in a very safe place. Soon he will be in the hands of people who are expert at gaining answers to difficult questions.'

'And I'll no doubt be handed over to your friends in the Gestapo.'

'Oh no, Hannay, I have something much better in mind for you.' There was in her voice an echo of that childish vindictiveness I had heard before. 'They would undoubtedly make you suffer prolonged questioning followed by a firing squad or an eternity starving in some obscure dungeon. But you and I have a private score to settle and I will let nothing interfere with that.'

My temper rose. 'If you want to shoot me, why don't you get on with it?' I said. 'I'm growing tired of your nasty little games.'

'To shoot you would be to give you a soldier's death, which would be too much to your liking.' Her mouth distorted into an ugly smirk. 'No, I will not grant you that dignity. Your death will be slow and ignominious. You will breath out your last in solitary darkness, knowing that your own rashness carried you straight into my waiting hands.'

The deep, disfiguring scars on her soul were becoming more and more evident, and I began to wonder what sort of a war such wickedness was leading us all into.

'You know,' I said, 'there was a time when your people, for all their misdeeds, were capable of a degree of magnanimity, when most of them still recognised what was decent and what was not.'

'There is a new Germany now,' Beata declared proudly, 'capable of bold action that lies beyond the bounds of your imagination. You are too much of a *gentleman* to conceive of such things. Even now, the racially impure, the depraved and the disabled are being erased so completely that future generations will not even know they existed.'

'I suppose all this is to clear the way for the superman we hear so much about,' I said. 'Frankly he sounds to me like a bit of a swine.'

'How limited you are,' she sneered, 'stuck away on your little island reminiscing about your past glories over your port and cigars. I suppose you must view me as some sort of monster.'

With an effort I shook my head. 'You are a child orphaned by war seeking empty revenge against a world that has treated you cruelly. I feel sorry for you.'

She moved so quickly in her fury that I was taken by surprise when she lashed the back of her hand across my face.

Leaning closer, she said, 'Save your pity for yourself, Hannay. The world is no longer a place where you *good old chaps* are fit to survive. You will be swept away along with your titles, your country houses and your empty-headed wives serving afternoon tea.'

My cheek burned like the devil but I managed a hoarse chuckle. 'Clearly you've never met my wife.'

That small act of violence appeared to calm Beata and she regained her self-possession.

'When we searched you we found little of interest.' From the table to her right she picked up my copy of *The Pilgrim's Progress*. She flicked disinterestedly through the pages, her lips curled in mockery. 'And what is this?' she asked, waving it in front of my face. 'Some sort of religious tract?'

'I suppose that's all it could be. To you.'

'How pitiful.' She slipped the book into my jacket pocket. 'Here, you can keep it. When you die you can take your god with you.'

'What are you going to do?' I asked. 'Bury me alive? I've never been a fan of Mr Poe and his rather fevered imaginings.'

'In these final days many people have thrown their valuables into the Seine to keep them out of the reach of the invaders,' Beata explained in an amused tone. 'How foolishly people behave when their civilisation is coming to a close. That is your fate, Hannay: to be locked inside a wooden box and thrown into the river. You will be no more than a piece of discarded furniture sinking to the bottom of the Seine.'

She opened the door and called out. In answer to her summons two burly, stone-faced men, still dressed as waiters, came to drag me away to my execution.

'As the river seeps in you will feel your death approaching with a chilling inevitability,' Beata told me. 'For a man such as you, to drown like this, unseen and unknown, will be the worst possible death.'

16

THE ORACLE

I was still too weak from the drug to put up any sort of fight as they released me from the chair and pulled me roughly to my feet. They bound my arms behind me while Beata watched dispassionately, as though this were merely a piece of routine business. Only the intensity with which she drew in the smoke from her cigarette betrayed her depth of feeling.

As her lackeys bundled me through the door my thoughts were racing. How had she learned of her mother's fate? I could only suppose some survivor of that battle had carried the tale back to Germany with much heroic elaboration and passed it on to the orphaned child. Whatever were the bare facts of her mother's end, she must have grown up with a version magnified through the lens of heroic myth. Sandy, Blenkiron and myself had been reduced to the status of black-hearted troglodytes who had undone both a noble life and the promise of a magnificent destiny.

Beata followed as her servants hauled me up to a room adjoining the entrance hall where a plain armoire, not even an antique, had been laid flat on the floor, its door yawning open to welcome me. My ankles were quickly bound together and my mouth stuffed with a gag, then my captors hoisted me up and lowered me into my casket. Beata stretched out an elegant leg to kick the door shut with the toe of her expensive high-heeled shoe.

Plunged into a musty darkness, I heard the click of a key in the lock. The armoire was shifted upright and loaded onto some sort of trolley, then, wheels squeaking, we were on the move, trundling through the house. I saw no point in making any sort of difficulty while we were indoors, but perhaps, once we were out in the street, there might be a passer-by to notice any sort of ruckus I might make.

Doors opened and closed, carpets gave way to bare floor, then came a series of bumps as we descended the front steps to cross the courtyard. I heard the door in the outer wall open and I was tilted from side to side as Beata's henchmen manoeuvred the heavy box out onto the pavement.

At this point I began flinging my weight around as far as the constricted space would allow. My sole hope was that my casket would fall and split apart on impact. Even then, unless there were somebody to witness the event, I would only be forcing my enemies to put an end to me more swiftly, but it was still worth the chance.

My captors did not lose their grip, however. I heard one of them curse in German, branding me the Teutonic equivalent of a bloody nuisance, as they persevered in their grim work. My head jarred as the top of the armoire was loaded into a vehicle then shoved in the whole way. Doors slammed shut, an engine growled, and off we went up the Rue Vaneau.

Trapped in darkness, I reflected on what I had learned. Clearly Beata van Diemen had a number of agents in her employ. How easy it must have been for them to slip into Paris among the streams of refugees and then assume the role of servants in her great house. I knew for certain also that Roland was indeed a prisoner of these enemy spies, just as Blenkiron had surmised. And yet how futile this information now was.

It was not the dread of death but the sense of failure and futility that oppressed me. I had been in enough battles, faced enough hazards, not to be overly anxious about my own survival. I had, after all, lived a life fuller than most, and it was some consolation to be making my exit as a player in the great game, not as a forgotten man left to rot in enforced retirement. But, oh, to go like this, without even being able to take a swing at my captors, not even to cry out.

I wished there were some way I could get word to Jaikie and the others, to let them know I had come within reach of our goal. I could only hope that they had found some path of their own that would yet lead to the success of our mission and that they would not be blinded as I had been by the beauty and brilliance of our enemy.

Overwhelming all of these thoughts, however, were images of Mary – as she had been when we first met in the garden at Fosse so many years ago, as she was on our last night together when we held each other so close our two heartbeats became one. In a marriage such as ours nothing had been left unsaid, but I would have risked my chance of Heaven to be able to say it all again one more time.

The drive to the Seine was too brief for any further reflection. The van stopped, the doors opened, and my captors hauled the armoire out onto the trolley. I threw myself about as violently as possible but the space was too restricted to gain any sort of purchase. I heard the squeak of the wheels and felt myself being conveyed down a stone ramp to a riverside embankment.

When we halted I heard the two Germans grunt as they lifted the armoire and prepared to heave it into the water. There seemed nothing left to do but pray in darkness and silence that some good might come from my sacrifice, that I had perhaps shaken the intentions of our enemies sufficiently to give Jaikie and the others some opportunity to frustrate their plans.

In a final flush of frustration, I rolled about from side to side and kicked my feet as best I could, determined to be no passive victim even at the end. I knew only seconds were left to me – but then came an unexpected uproar.

Angry voices rang out amid the sounds of a scuffle. My captors let the armoire fall and it struck the paving below with an impact that knocked the air from my lungs. I could hear blows being struck and curses exchanged, bodies bumping against my casket, then came a sudden silence.

I was still recovering my breath when somebody outside smashed the lock on the armoire with one stroke of some heavy object. The door was flung open, but there was no dramatic inpouring of light, for dawn was only just breaking. Silhouetted against the gloom, two faces peered in at me. It was only when one of them leaned down to loosen my gag that I recognised them.

'Well, that was a bit of a close call, sir,' said Jaikie, tossing away the rag.

'We've cut it fine ourselves sometimes,' Dougal agreed, 'but never as fine as this. If Jaikie hadn't got into the midst of them as fast as a wildcat, you'd have been in the drink.'

I worked the stiffness out of my jaw enough to say thanks.

'I think you were making it awkward for them to keep a grip, sir,' said Jaikie, 'which was enough of a distraction to let us surprise them.'

They cut my bonds and helped me to my feet, lending me much needed support as I stepped out of my wooden prison. Beata's two men were laid out flat, dazed and groaning from the Die-Hards' assault. Peter stood over them with a pistol in case they showed any sign of causing trouble. Thomas was at the top of the embankment keeping a lookout.

'We'd best wrap this up,' he advised.

'Right, we need to move,' said Dougal, 'because these rogues have a whole army coming to their aid.'

I was still shaking off the effects of the sedative and recovering from the stiffness of my captivity as I mumbled, 'Roland, we can't go without Roland.'

'First things first,' said Dougal, taking charge of our two captives.

The Die-Hards pushed them at gunpoint up to where they had parked the van. Tying them together with the same bonds that had held me they gagged both men. The Germans were then laid out flat on the floor of the van.

'Now, mind,' Dougal warned them, 'if we hear any noise out of you, we'll have to come and shoot you.' He repeated the threat in German, which made it sound even more menacing, then slammed the door on the prisoners.

Jaikie kept a hand under my elbow to steady me as we hurried over to the Delage which was parked nearby. A wan grey light was seeping up the horizon, silhouetting the town houses and stately monuments of Paris. The quiet was extraordinary, but it was not the peaceful calm of the waking day – it was the stillness of a graveyard in the hour before a funeral begins.

In his capacity as our medic, Peter gave me a quick once-over and handed me a flask of water. I drank thirstily, washing the bad taste out of my mouth. 'How did you find me?'

'Mr Blenkiron told me it was your habit to plunge in where the danger was fiercest and stagger out of the smoke and flames with the prize in your hands,' said Jaikie.

I leaned unsteadily against the bonnet of the car. 'If it were only that simple,' I told him ruefully.

'Well, bearing that in mind, when you didn't return from your party, we thought it wise to head down to the Rue Vaneau and keep an eye out for you.'

'And catch me when I came staggering out.'

Jaikie allowed himself the slightest of smiles. 'Except you didn't. The other guests all left singly or in groups, but there was no sign of you. Peter thought you might have sneaked out in disguise.'

'Having heard something of your reputation, sir,' Peter explained, 'that was a possibility.'

'But I was pretty sure I'd recognise you,' Jaikie interjected, 'even if that were the case.'

'So it was as plain as day that you'd fallen into enemy hands,' Dougal concluded. 'I said we should storm the place and take our chances.'

'I was for playing it canny,' said Jaikie, 'and Thomas backed me up.'

The pastor inclined his head in acknowledgement. 'When the game is still in the balance,' he said, 'it's plain daft to coup over the board.'

'So we kept watch,' said Dougal grimly, 'galling as it was to be twiddling our thumbs.'

I gathered there had been an impassioned debate among the Die-Hards that had left some heat behind it.

'When these men came heaving an armoire out of the house into the back of the van, I had a hunch we'd spotted our man,' said Jaikie.

'From the way they were labouring,' said Peter, 'it was ower heavy to be empty.'

'And it was definitely a queer business to be flitting furniture about in the hour before dawn,' Dougal added. 'Aye, the waiting game seemed to have paid off.'

As succinctly as I could I filled them in on what had happened. 'Did you see Beata leave the house?' I asked.

'We had to follow that van as quick as we could,' said Dougal, 'and it didn't strike me as wise to divide our forces.'

'Will she not be back at the house to keep an eye on this Roland fellow?' said Peter.

I shook my head, which hurt as if my brain were coming loose. 'He's not there, and I expect she and the rest of her men have gone to stand guard over him. They're bound to suspect that I'm not here alone and that there are others out to free their captive.'

'I don't suppose she let slip where she's got him stashed?' said Jaikie.

I thought back, doing my best to recall Beata's exact words. 'She referred to him as an item and said that he was stored in a safe place, almost as if he were a piece of antique merchandise.'

Jaikie's brow knotted. 'And where does that take us?'

Turning over in my mind what Bullitt had told me of Beata, I had a sudden glimmer of intuition. 'I was told that one of her public occupations was as a dealer in antiques,' I said. 'As such she must have a place of business where valuable items are kept.'

'I see where you're going with this,' Dougal growled, 'but how are we supposed to find it?'

'Perhaps we need the help of a good book,' Thomas suggested.

'With the best will in the world, Thomas,' said Peter, 'this is hardly the time to be seeking inspiration from the Bible.'

'I wasn't speaking about that good book,' said Thomas. He reached into the back of the car and produced a small russet volume. 'I meant this one.'

Jaikie peered at it. 'A Paris business directory?'

'I borrowed this, a phone book, and a few other items from the hotel,' Thomas explained, 'in case they should prove useful in our travels.'

'I swear you are the most practically-minded clergyman I've ever encountered,' I complimented him as I accepted the book.

I flipped through the pages to the section on antiques, searching for some trace of the name van Diemen. None of the business names resembled that, none of them were Dutch, nor did the name von Einem appear. I was about to cast the book aside in frustration when something did catch my eye.

'Le Pégase!' I exclaimed.

'What's that when it's at home?' Peter enquired.

'It's an antiques store in the Rue Bellardine,' I replied. 'And that name – I'll swear it's French for Pegasus.'

'The winged horse from the Greek myths?' said Jaikie.

'That's the place, I'm sure of it,' I told him with growing conviction. 'Quick, there's not a second to lose. I'll explain on the way.'

'If we're going into battle,' said Dougal, 'you'll be wanting this.'

He handed me my pistol and shoulder holster.

We piled into the car, picking out our route by the map Thomas had pulled from his pocket. I explained my reasoning to my companions, hoping that my instinct was correct.

I had felt at the time that Beata was taunting me when she drew attention to the brooch with the winged horse, but was it more than my helplessness she was mocking? Did it sweeten her sense of victory to dangle before me a clue to where she was holding Roland prisoner and only then to consign me to death? Whether consciously or otherwise, I was certain she had given me the lead we needed so badly.

Dougal drove at high speed, taking advantage of the fact that we were virtually the only traffic. Here and there I spotted a side street that had been blocked off with a lorry or a wagon. A few Parisians, I guessed, had put these obstacles in place as a token resistance against the invaders. After the cynical defeatism of last night's party, it was heartening to see at least a remnant of the fighting French spirit.

We parked out of sight of our destination, and Jaikie and I went on ahead to scout out the lie of the land. Keeping to the early morning shadows we made our way cautiously up the Rue Bellarmine. A large sign marked the place: *Le Pégase, Une Maison des Antiquités*. It was a large red brick building three storeys high with a stout front door flanked by barred windows.

'You wait here,' said Jaikie. 'I'll circle around and see what we're up against.'

He had no sooner spoken than he disappeared from view. I sank back well out of sight, for I was sure I spotted movement at the windows. I was suddenly alerted to a deep, distant buzzing, and when I looked up I saw a formation of German aircraft flying over the city. They separated, swooping low to reconnoitre the streets. My nerves tingled warningly as they passed overhead for I knew they were the heralds of the mighty army that would soon occupy the city.

A few minutes later Jaikie popped up again as if from nowhere. His expression was grim. 'We'd best get back to the others for a council of war,' he said.

The Die-Hards gathered eagerly around their scout and listened intently to his report.

'The delivery yard round the back was deserted so I sneaked in there and managed to jemmy open a window without being heard,' he told them. 'There's plenty of cover inside, what with the antique furniture and packing cases, so I made my way about pretty handily. I spotted at least half a dozen rough-looking types speaking to each other in German.'

He paused to glance at me before continuing. 'There was a blonde girl there, too, and she was obviously in charge. They were mostly clustered about a stairway leading down to the basement, so I guess that's where they've got their prisoner locked up.'

'So what's your assessment?' Dougal asked.

Jaikie shook his head. 'They're well armed and dug in as deep as a badger in his sett. It will take more firepower than we've got to root them out.'

'And once the German army gets here, any shooting's going to bring them running,' I added.

'It's pretty certain those lads mean to sit tight until their pals get here and there's nothing that will shift them in the meantime,' Dougal grumbled.

I was wondering if we simply had to chance making an assault, no matter how hopeless, when I noticed the eyes of the Die-Hards were all fixed on Thomas. From their expectant gaze you would have thought him an oracle who could divine the will of the gods.

Jaikie had told me that the pastor was the master strategist of the group in the rough days of their youth, but he presented a sober figure now, who was no longer the would-be pirate of boyhood.

Thomas's eyes were downcast in deep thought and I wondered whether the Die-Hards' confidence in his intelligence was founded upon youthful games rather than hard facts. However, when he looked up, there was a gleam in his eye that immediately dispelled my doubts. The guile of his youth had not abandoned him.

'Boys, there's only one answer,' he said, his Scottish burr becoming more pronounced with each word. 'We maun be the Germans.'

17

SCAVENGER HUNT

Thomas quickly outlined his plan, assigning to each of the Die-Hards his particular role. It was as brilliant as it was audacious, although even as I listened I dared not contemplate how slender the odds of success must be.

'Every one of you is an expert scrounger,' the pastor concluded, 'so chap on doors, break into shops if you have to, for we must be like the good thief and hope for forgiveness. We've no more than a half-hour's grace, so go to it!'

There followed the most remarkable scavenger hunt I have ever witnessed. I was left to guard the car and watch in growing admiration as one by one my young companions returned with their bounty. Dougal obtained a red sheet, a wooden pole and a pot of black paint with a brush. Thomas had bagged a loud-hailer and a pair of grey overcoats with matching caps. Jaikie came hurrying up the street with a wind-up phonograph cradled in his arms, swiftly followed by Peter with a collection of records.

'I had a sair fecht finding somebody that would admit to having these,' Peter declared with a grin, 'but I think they'll do the job.'

'Good work, boys,' Thomas complimented his friends. 'Now we must set to work.'

While the pastor shuffled through the records, Peter wound up the phonograph and Dougal began painting a large black swastika on the crimson sheet.

'It turns my stomach to do this,' he said sourly, 'but needs must.'

All of us paused momentarily, for our ears had picked up a warning sound – a low growl in some far-off street. From the north a line of military vehicles was advancing into the city. I remembered how, when I went to play on the beach, my mother always warned me to keep an eye out for the tide or I would find myself stranded on a sand bar. I knew that now a similarly inexorable tide would all too quickly engulf us.

Without a word being spoken, Jaikie and I checked our pistols, and I followed him on a stealthy course around to the loading yard at the back of the store.

'I doubt we'll have more than a couple of minutes,' he said, 'so we'll need to be nippy. Even if Thomas's scheme works as we hope, we'll still have a guard or two to deal with.'

'There will be no time for niceties,' I agreed. 'Anybody that stands in our way must go down fast and hard.'

Jaikie climbed onto a discarded packing case and peered through the window he had forced earlier. We had a short tense wait until we heard the Die-Hards go into action.

I knew from the plan that the Delage was passing along the street some distance off. The braying horns of Wagner's *Valkyrie* roared triumphantly from the phonograph while Dougal stood on the running board in a grey coat and cap he hoped would pass for a uniform to anyone who didn't get too close. Fluent as he was in both languages from his journalistic travels, he bellowed through the loud-hailer in alternating French and German: 'People of Paris, you have nothing to fear! This is your moment of liberation! You are now proud subjects of the Reich!'

It was Thomas's intention that with the flag waving above the car and the Die-Hards' rowdy demonstration of victory, Beata and her crew would be convinced that their fellow countrymen had arrived. With any luck, that distraction would buy Jaikie and me just enough time to make our move.

From inside the building I distinctly heard a raucous cheer. My heart leapt at this initial success, but I was well aware that the deception would not hold up indefinitely.

Jaikie climbed nimbly over the window ledge, signalling me to follow. We dropped inside and crouched low behind a pile of rolled-up Persian rugs. Beyond lay a capacious storage area that covered the entire ground floor, packed from end to end with statues, paintings, furniture and ornaments, most of them covered or boxed up. It was clear that while her fellow antique dealers were fleeing the city in a panic, Beata had picked up any number of bargains.

Jaikie and I made our way forward, dodging from cover to cover, drawing ever closer to the stairway. Beata and her men were moving towards the front and we saw an oblong of light appear as the guard there threw open the door.

The Germans spilled onto the street and cried out boisterously to the figures in the car, welcoming them to Paris and promising them a delightful time. Their bogus compatriots, I guessed, were waving back enthusiastically while being careful to keep their distance.

Only one man had been left behind to guard the steps down to the cellar. With a sub-machine gun cradled in his arms, he was staring at his comrades, clearly wishing he could rush out and join the celebration. He tapped his foot on the floor in time to Wagner's warlike music.

In an open packing case near at hand lay a bronze statuette of the goddess Aphrodite. Snatching her from her cradle of straw, I crept up on the guard from behind. Before he could turn around, I swung the statuette like a cricket bat at his head. My makeshift club connected solidly over his left ear and he dropped like a felled ox with blood welling from his temple.

The din from outside covered the noise of our encounter. Jaikie darted forward and snatched the sub-machine gun from the guard's limp fingers. Stooping, I ransacked his pockets and pulled out a set of keys.

To our right lay a flight of stairs connecting with the cellar. On my signal, Jaikie took up a guard position facing the outer door while I descended the steps. Below lay three doors, but only one of them was shut. I rifled swiftly through the keys till I found the right one and yanked the door open.

Light from the hallway poured into a bare, darkened room beyond. In the far corner crouched a dishevelled figure in a grubby shirt and torn trousers. He lurched to his feet, holding up a hand to shield his eyes from the glare.

'Roland?'

After an uncertain pause, he nodded. I could see he was taken aback by the sudden appearance of a stranger, and made haste to reassure him. 'I'm a friend,' I told him. 'I've come to get you out of here. We must be quick.'

When he stumbled out into the light I could see he was barely thirty years old with wavy chestnut hair, a strong chin and keen hazel eyes. There were shocking bruises on his face, and he winced as he moved, evidence of the rough treatment he had received at the hands of his captors. The prospect of freedom, however, lent him a jolt of energy and he bounded up the stairway close behind me.

'Gabriel!' Jaikie exclaimed as soon as he caught sight of the captive. 'What a bonnie sight you are!'

The freed man's eyes widened in incredulous recognition. 'Jaikie! What on earth are you doing here?'

'No time to explain now,' said Jaikie. 'Sir Richard Hannay, this is Graf Gabriel von Falken.'

His friend raised a reproving hand. 'Jaikie, you know we don't use those titles in Austria any more. It is plain Gabriel Falken, just as it was at Cambridge.'

The reunion of the old college friends was cut short by a spatter of gunfire from the street. The Germans had seen through the trick and opened up on the Die-Hards who immediately returned fire. I heard Beata's voice berating her minions with the viciousness of a harpy.

A clatter of booted feet warned us that some of them were hurrying back towards us in response to Beata's shrieked command. She understood at once the purpose of the diversion and she had no intention of letting her prize slip from her grasp.

Jaikie fired off a scatter of bullets that sent the Germans diving to the ground. Beata melted into the shadows and snapped off a couple of shots that whizzed by Jaikie's ear, forcing him back into cover.

'I'll hold them off, sir,' he gasped. 'You get Gabriel out of here.'

There was no time for me to argue or to thank him. Seizing Gabriel by the sleeve, I yanked him after me and dashed for the rear window. I felt rotten about leaving Jaikie and the others behind to fight it out, but my mission was clear: I was to get Gabriel out of here and back to London, if that was at all possible.

I boosted him up through the window ahead of me and clambered out behind him into the yard. Before the Germans could think to cut off the rear, we raced for the lane beyond.

From behind us came the rumble of military vehicles and a sharp increase in gunfire. Wehrmacht troops had arrived to rendezvous with Beata and were now engaged in a firefight with the Die-Hards.

As Gabriel and I pelted down the lane, a window above us was flung open by a beefy man who shook his fist angrily while unleashing a stream of obscenities. In the heat of the moment, I couldn't tell if he was cursing the Germans or merely complaining about having his sleep disturbed.

As we approached the main road the growl of heavy engines ahead brought us to a halt. Ducking behind a corner, I saw that the newly arrived Germans were methodically sweeping the streets. My heart sank: it was only a matter of time before we were surrounded and cut off.

Gabriel suddenly placed a firm hand on my shoulder and I could tell that he had quite shaken off the enfeebling effects of his captivity. There was a determined glint in his eye that told me for the first time that he was indeed a man upon whom the future fate of Europe might well depend.

'Sir Richard, I must ask you to trust me,' he said in the voice of one used to taking command of a bad situation. 'I believe I can get us to safety, but we must move rapidly and you must ask no questions.'

'Lead on,' I urged him.

Crouching low and keeping to whatever cover he could find, he led me down a series of streets and alleyways with an unhesitating confidence that told me he had the whole city mapped out in his head. When we heard hoof beats ahead, we dropped out of sight behind a stationary car. A German trooper with a rifle slung over his back came riding down the street on a grey gelding, his eyes darting from side to side. As soon as he was past, we resumed our progress.

'I have made some friendly contacts in Paris,' Gabriel assured me. 'They have not all proved as treacherous as Beata van Diemen.'

We came to a low wall. Gabriel climbed on top and offered a hand to haul me up beside him. We dropped down into a fragrant garden of rose bushes and hyacinth beds. Among the flowers stood a statue of Jesus touching a hand to his sacred heart. Beyond lay a simple stone building surmounted by a cross and a bell tower. From inside came the faintest sound of female voices raised in song.

'Have I misunderstood,' I asked my companion, 'or are we breaking into a convent?'

'Not breaking in exactly,' said Gabriel as we halted by a small back door.

He tugged once on the bell pull, waited a few seconds, rang twice, then after a few moments rang a further three times. Following an anxious wait, the door opened a crack and the face of a young girl encircled by a nun's wimple peered out at us. At the sight of Gabriel she waved us inside, closing and locking the door behind us.

'Restez ici,' she instructed us before disappearing down the narrow corridor.

Barely seconds later we were joined by another nun, a much older woman, whose sharp cheekbones and narrow mouth were softened by warm brown eyes that regarded us with kindness and concern.

'Monsieur Roland,' she greeted my companion.

Without bothering to introduce me, he said, 'Mother Véronique, we need refuge – for a short time only, I swear.'

'Yes, we have heard the Boche in the streets,' she said, her face souring in distaste. 'Come with me.'

She led us silently through the dimly lit passageways of the convent. As we passed the doorway of the chapel I could hear from within the voices of the sisters raised in a heartfelt prayer to the Queen of Heaven.

'*Sancta Maria, Mater Dei, ora pro nobis peccatoribus nunc et in hora mortis nostrae. Amen.*'

We entered the mother superior's office where two vases of blue and yellow flowers presented an odd contrast to the stark image of the suffering Christ that hung from the wall. In the better light Mother Véronique noticed the bruises on Gabriel's face. She tutted like an anxious parent and offered to fetch some ointment, but my companion insisted that we go into hiding at once.

The nun instructed us to move her desk a few feet forward then she tugged aside the rug that lay beneath. There was a trapdoor with an iron ring which Gabriel grabbed to pull it open.

Mother Véronique lit an oil lantern and handed it to me. She murmured a prayer over us as I followed my companion down a narrow wooden stairway to a cramped cellar. The trapdoor closed behind us and we heard the rug and the desk being shifted back into position.

The cellar was sparsely furnished with a pair of wooden chairs. Once we were seated Gabriel glanced upward and said, 'We should be safe here, sir, until the Germans move on.'

A thousand questions clamoured in my head but I restrained them for the moment. 'I won't call you Graf von Falken if you don't call me sir,' I suggested.

Gabriel nodded his agreement. 'After the last war, with the end of the Hapsburgs, all such titles were banned in Austria, though some of the old nobility still use them when abroad. So, Richard it is. And I am Gabriel.'

'Well, Gabriel,' I said with a weary smile, 'now that we're friends, perhaps you can tell me something about these thirty-one kings that we're all risking our lives for.'

18

A MATTER OF KINGS

———

'Yes, the thirty-one kings,' said Gabriel. He paused, brow furrowed, as if he were gathering his thoughts.

I remained silent and after a moment he began his account.

'When I was at Cambridge with our friend Jaikie,' he began, 'history was my great passion. Not the sort of history that interests you English. If you don't mind my saying so, for you it seems to consist of memorising the names and dates of your own kings and queens and talking endlessly about the Battle of Hastings, you know, ten sixty-six and such like.'

'I think you're doing us a bit of a disservice,' I interpolated drily, 'but do go on.'

Gabriel conceded the point with a small gesture of apology. His eyes, however, were fixed on a larger vision when he continued. 'I have studied the rise and fall of civilisations, the spread of empires both good and bad, and this has given me a certain perspective. I cannot see the events of my own time in isolation. Every uprising, every crisis, grows out of what has gone before and, more than that, presages future events, if we could but read the meaning.'

'Reading a meaning into the past is common enough,' I said, 'but predicting the future has never been more than empty speculation.'

'Perhaps so, but we must make the effort to see where history is leading us,' said Gabriel in a scholarly tone, 'and consider what steps we must take if the disasters of a previous age are not to overwhelm us again.'

'That would be a nice trick if you could pull it off,' I agreed.

Gabriel leaned forward intently, the pale glow of the lantern upon his face lending him the appearance of an ancient sage or storyteller hunched over a camp fire with a circle of followers gathered about him.

'You will recall, Richard, that during the Dark Ages, after Rome had fallen to the barbarians, the light of knowledge was kept alive by a network of monasteries.'

'I'm not quite that old, but I do remember reading about it.'

This prompted the first smile I had seen from this earnest young man in our short but eventful acquaintance. The smile faded as he resumed.

'Through that dark age those monks copied out innumerable manuscripts, preserving the knowledge of antiquity – science, philosophy and the arts – until civilisation dawned once more under the rule of Charlemagne, the first of the Holy Roman Emperors.'

He paused for a moment and I began to wonder what this history lesson of his was building up to.

'Now the barbarians are back' – Gabriel's mouth tightened – 'and two years ago they occupied Vienna, the last seat of the Holy Roman Empire. There was a time when my people looked favourably upon the idea of a union with our kinsfolk in Germany, even though it was forbidden by the Treaty of Versailles.'

'Anything that has been forbidden by others will always have a certain appeal, I suppose.'

Gabriel's expression grew even more sombre. 'Well, that changed with the coming of Hitler and his thugs. The nature of such a union now looked very different, as it would amount simply to an annexation of our country. When Hitler's supporters in the Austrian Nazi party assassinated our prime minister a few years ago, many of us saw what was coming. The fall of Paris, along with all that she represents, is just another step in the resurgence of the new barbarism. Some of us realised from the beginning that the brutal regime in Berlin was no passing fluke of history, but the beginning of a new dark age.'

In spite of myself I was deeply struck by the stark prospect he presented. I said uneasily, 'I hear the Führer thinks his empire will last a thousand years.'

Gabriel nodded grimly. 'If it takes root it might well do so. That is why there must be resistance everywhere, no matter how hopeless it appears, no matter what the cost. To this end I have spent the last five years travelling under a series of assumed names, making contacts with underground dissenters, organising such groups where there were none.'

I could not help but be impressed – awed almost – by the magnitude of the task he had set himself. 'So you're saying that you have created a network of secret monasteries to resist the darkness.'

'Many have been involved' – Gabriel raised a self-deprecating hand – 'and many have risked far greater dangers than I, but yes, it exists. They must keep alive the very idea of freedom – the knowledge that obedience is not a necessity and that power is not righteousness.'

'And this is what you refer to as the thirty-one kings?'

'There are many more than thirty-one of them, and they come from all walks of life, but that is the name we assigned to this project.'

'From what you say it must be a huge operation.'

A taut smile crossed Gabriel's lips. 'We have agents all across Europe, Richard, a silent army, stretching from Warsaw to Athens, from Paris to Belgrade. Already they are gathering intelligence to pass on to your military and planning acts of sabotage. Many have even armed themselves for a future uprising. The individual groups are unknown to each other, so that they must be coordinated by code names and passwords – all of which exist only here.' He tapped his temple.

Now that I knew the truth, I felt in its fullness all the weight of the responsibility I bore for this young man's safety. 'I can see why the Germans are so keen to get their hands on you. If they had that information, they could use it to flush out these cells.'

Gabriel laid an urgent hand on my arm. 'It is vitally important that I deliver this information to your government, to give them the means to contact the many allies they have in the occupied nations. And in Germany itself.'

'Plans are in place,' I assured him. 'Once we get out of here, we're to make our way to Bordeaux. There's a rendezvous point there where transport to London will be arranged.'

Gabriel's grip tightened. 'It is just as vital that a message be sent to the whole of this unseen army to tell them that their efforts will not be in vain, that the British will fight on until Europe is liberated, however long it takes. They must know that even in the midst of this all-consuming darkness they have not been abandoned.'

In his haunted eyes I glimpsed the bleak vision that had driven him these past five years. Cooped up as we were in this little bolthole, I felt I should attempt to lighten his burden, if only for the time being.

'I hope *we* haven't been abandoned,' I joked. 'I have to say I'm getting pretty peckish.'

Gabriel's expression lightened. He removed his hand from my arm and managed a chuckle. 'Mother Véronique will take good care of us. You can be very sure of that.'

He explained how only days ago one of the fleeing refugees she had helped had put him in contact with Beata van Diemen. Too late he learned her true nature and her true mission.

I was telling him of my encounter with that terrible and alluring young woman when we were interrupted by a scuffling from above. It was the sound of the desk being moved. Instinctively I drew my pistol, ready to shoot if the enemy had cornered us. Then came a precise sequence of knocks. Gabriel pressed my gun down with the palm of his hand and shook his head to indicate that there was no danger.

The trapdoor swung open and we climbed out to meet Mother Véronique who directed us to a tray of coffee and buttered croissants. The younger sister was also present with overcoats and hats for us which we slipped on while bolting our breakfast.

'The streets are clear for now,' the mother superior informed us, 'but you must escape before they can close a cordon around the city.'

'My car is ready?' asked Gabriel.

Wordlessly Mother Véronique reached into the folds of her habit and handed him a set of keys. He thanked her and we washed down our breakfast with a few last gulps of coffee. The nuns escorted us to the back door and we scurried across the garden.

Once we were over the wall, Gabriel led the way with the same sure confidence as before. The streets were free of the enemy, though from the distance we could hear a rumble of engines and the drone of aircraft. I trusted that the Die-Hards had led our pursuers on a merry chase and I hoped the courage and resourcefulness of the four Glasgow lads would take them safely out of Paris. However, that was out of my hands. My business was to get Gabriel away, though for the present he was doing a fine job of taking command.

He led me to a small garage tucked away at the back of a coal merchant's yard. Gabriel unlocked the sliding metal door and opened it to reveal a compact Peugeot saloon. Wasting not one precious second, we jumped in. Gabriel started her up and we set off at high speed. There was so little traffic nothing impeded us from racing south and west to the outskirts of Paris.

'Beata may be determined to capture us,' said Gabriel, 'but the priority of the German military is to occupy the key strategic points across the city. That is a time-consuming process and their full strength will not arrive until later in the day.'

I hoped his assessment was correct and that Beata's resources for search and pursuit would be severely limited.

The large cosmopolitan buildings gave way to a suburban spread of modest houses and streets dotted with poplars and sycamores. Even here almost no one was venturing out of doors. It was as if the whole of Paris were holding its breath, waiting to discover what the nature of the occupation would be.

We were beginning to think we had eluded the occupying forces when we spotted a military lorry marked with the Teutonic cross obstructing the road ahead. A dozen soldiers had disembarked and one of them barked out a challenge when he saw us coming at high speed.

He raised his rifle and fired a warning shot. At the same moment Gabriel gave the wheel a violent twist. More shots sounded as we swerved into an adjoining street. Such was our haste that we didn't spot we were heading into more trouble until it was too late.

Someone had spread oil across the street, not to trap us but to inconvenience the hated invaders. That small act of defiance was our undoing. When we hit the slick we were thrown into an uncontrollable spin and Gabriel spat out an uncharacteristic curse in his native tongue.

He braked hard but could not keep us from skidding giddily across the road until our rear bashed into a cherry tree and we jolted to a stop. Both of us rebounded off the dashboard, and it took us a few moments to gather ourselves.

When we came to our senses we found that we were surrounded by the enemy.

19

THE HOST OF HEAVEN

––––

Our captors marched us to a nearby school building that was being transformed into a makeshift barracks. Consigned to the janitor's room, we were seated on a wooden bench with our backs against the wall. Gabriel and I assessed the quality of the twenty-odd soldiers stationed here. They looked young and relatively untried, but knowing how rigorously the new Reich drilled its men, that was no reason to underestimate them.

Their fresh-faced officer was in something of a quandary over what to do with us. It was plain that we were a nuisance and he had more than enough to keep him busy without a pair of unwanted prisoners. He was, however, in some fear of letting us go in case we turned out to be saboteurs or some other kind of wanted fugitives.

We had no means of identification as both of us had been deprived of such documents by Beata van Diemen, but this left us free to pass ourselves off as Frenchmen. I told the officer I was a watchmaker named Aristide Villon and that Gabriel was my son, Jacques. Gabriel was sharp enough to follow my lead as I spun a yarn about fetching him from the city to visit his sick mother. She was not expected to last the morning, which was why he had been driving with such reckless haste and why we had both rushed out without any form of identification. It was harder to explain my pistol, but I said I was in fear of the looters and brigands I had heard were roaming the streets of Paris.

The young officer had only a basic command of French, so it was not difficult for us to pass ourselves off as natives. It also made it awkward for him to question us in any detail about why neither of us had as much as a wallet on our persons or how I had obtained my pistol. He departed with a scowl, leaving us under guard while he radioed for instructions and passed on a detailed description of us both to his central command.

Assessing the number of troops around us, and the fact that they were all nervously alert during these first few hours in the conquered city, it was clear that our chances of making a run for it were almost non-existent – especially as we now had no means of transport. In fact, I had the feeling that if we were shot while trying to escape, it would relieve our custodians of an irksome burden.

From the conversation I picked up among these soldiers, I gathered that what had brought them here was a report that one of their own pilots, downed a few days earlier, was hiding out in a sympathetic household in this district. If not for this perverse twist of fate we might well have found our route wide open. The sight of someone attempting to flee the city at this late stage was, however, immediately suspicious and it was only a matter of time before some line of dots was joined up between this small unit and Beata, who was no doubt in vengeful pursuit.

Gabriel and I discussed our situation in muted French, satisfied that our guard was too bored to take any interest in our mutterings.

'Richard,' said Gabriel anxiously, 'if you should get the chance to kill me you must take it.'

I had been racking my brains for an escape strategy and his request came as a shock.

'What on earth are you talking about?'

'Look, if they turn us over to the Gestapo, which I feel is inevitable, they have drugs and methods of torture that might force from me the very information they want, no matter how much I try to resist. That would be a disaster. Many lives would be lost, and all means of communication between your government and the thirty-one kings would be lost.'

It was clear to me that after days of apparently hopeless captivity, to be recaptured after so brief a period of freedom had left my young friend slightly overwrought.

'Gabriel,' I said in a calm voice calculated to steady him, 'you can't seriously expect me to do such a thing.'

His steadfast hazel eyes met mine. 'I would do it myself if the chance came, except that I can't. It goes directly against my faith.'

'In that case you should listen to your faith,' I told him firmly. 'Doesn't it instruct you that you must never abandon hope?'

He was silent for a few moments and I hoped that was a sign he was recovering his nerve. 'You're right, of course,' he agreed in a voice much more like his own, 'but it's hard to see any way out.'

'As long as we stay alive,' I told him, 'we're giving Providence a chance to do its work.'

He managed a weak smile. 'I expect you have some experience of that.'

'More than I can tell you. You hang on and one day I'll share a few stories with you.'

We fell silent when we saw the officer marching back towards us. 'A vehicle is being sent for you,' he informed us in halting French. 'You will be taken to the proper authorities. If you try to escape you will be shot.'

We nodded to indicate that we understood. He rapped out additional orders to the guard before returning to his other duties. The guard gave us a hard look and pressed a finger to his lips to inform us that conversation was now forbidden.

We sat in strained silence, watching for his attention to wander, but if we as much as shuffled our feet, he uttered a threatening grunt and brought his rifle to bear. I had the sense that he was disappointed at the absence of resistance in Paris and would be only too glad of the excuse to open fire on the enemy, even a pair of unarmed civilians sitting on a bench.

A mere twenty minutes later our new keepers arrived, and it was a sight as ugly as the gargoyles of Notre-Dame: an SS major and two tough-looking troopers. The major was slight of build, but his black uniform was as stiff as a suit of armour and from beneath the peak of his cap eyes as cold as a serpent's fixed upon us through rimless spectacles. His mouth was contorted and there was a stoop to his left shoulder that suggested some injury sustained in battle. His voice was just as disfigured, a harsh clatter of words that sounded like two pieces of flint striking off each other.

At his command his two brutish subordinates cuffed our hands behind us and ushered us at gunpoint to a waiting staff car, an open-topped Daimler flying a swastika from the bonnet. We were bundled into the back and one of the soldiers pressed in between Gabriel and the door.

The officer slid into the passenger seat and addressed us in his grating voice. 'I should advise you to attempt nothing rash. Corporal Schütz is an expert in every form of unarmed combat. I have seen him break a man's neck with only one hand.'

Leaving us to digest this disturbing information, he rapped out an order to the driver and the Daimler's big engine roared into life. I did not hear him mention a specific destination and concluded that it must have been arranged beforehand. Nevertheless I was surprised to see that we were not headed directly into the centre of Paris.

Instead we were cutting eastwards across the southern edge of the city. I speculated unhappily that we were being taken to a staging area from which we would be sent on to Germany, possibly by train. It was there that our true ordeal would begin.

'Please, I don't know who you think we are,' I said in my mildest German, 'but this is really a big mistake. I would advise you to take us to the American or Swiss embassy or you will be provoking a serious diplomatic incident.'

Without looking round, the major snapped an order to Schütz who reached out and smacked me hard in the mouth with the back of his hand. I felt blood trickling from my lip and judged that our new captor was in no mood for small talk. I glanced at Gabriel who was doing all he could to contain his anguish, but I knew that inside he was torn apart with fear for the brave men and women spread across the whole of Europe who had entrusted their future to him.

We pulled up in a barren stretch of wasteland surrounded by derelict buildings and rickety wooden sheds. The utter desolation of the place suggested only one reason for coming here, which was confirmed when we were ordered out of the car at the point of a rifle. This could only mean that we faced summary execution.

The two subordinates stood aside as the major drew his pistol and prepared to deal with us personally. We met his snakelike gaze squarely and I saw no glimmer of conscience or compunction there.

'I am well aware of your true identities,' he told us in fluent English. 'You are enemies of the Reich and for all such as you there can be only one penalty.'

I was utterly baffled by this turn of events. If he knew Gabriel's identity he was surely aware of the vital information he carried in his head.

Gabriel, however, looked at peace now. A silent grave was a preferable fate to weeks of torture and the possible betrayal of the thirty-one kings.

'Richard, I am sorry it must end like this,' he said hoarsely. 'Thank you for coming for me.'

'It's not the end, you know,' I assured him. 'As long as brave men are willing to die for something decent and honest, these brutes will never win.'

The major's next words came as a complete shock.

'I agree,' he said.

He turned his gun to the chest of the nearest trooper and pulled the trigger, blasting him straight through the heart. Before the other man could react he put a bullet into him and both men dropped lifeless onto the bare ground.

I would not have been more stunned if the host of Heaven had descended from the sky to land in our midst. I gawped at the major who was holstering his pistol.

The twist in his mouth was smoothed away, erasing the disdainful grimace that had given his features such an ugly cast. As he removed his glasses an impish twinkle lit his brown eyes and his face softened into one I recognised only too well. It was as boyish as ever in spite of the passage of so many years.

'Sandy!' I exclaimed. 'Dear God, man! How?'

As soon as he released us from our handcuffs I clamped my hands to his shoulders as if to convince myself that he was real and not an apparition conjured up out of my wildest, most impossible hopes.

Sandy's smile was like a burst of sunlight dispelling the last shreds of doom and confusion that had gripped me only moments before.

'To be honest, Dick, I think we have the same guardian angel and he's a very busy chap. It probably makes his job a little easier to keep bringing us together so we can look out for each other.'

Gabriel appeared utterly dumbfounded.

'Gabriel,' I explained, 'this is my dear old friend Sandy – Lord Clanroyden. If any stubborn Presbyterian ever tells you the age of miracles is long past, you be sure to tell them about this.'

I noticed that Sandy was gazing down at the two fallen SS troopers with genuine sorrow in his face.

'It feels damned cowardly killing them like that,' he sighed, 'but trying to subdue men as tough as these would have been a stupid risk.'

Gabriel was eyeing him with wonder. 'I have heard of you, of course, Lord Clanroyden, but I still find it hard to credit how thoroughly you have infiltrated the enemy.'

'The real Major Gantz had an unfortunate accident over a year ago,' said Sandy, 'which I had a hand in arranging. The moment he disappeared I stepped into his place. He was not a family man and had few friends, plus he had just been reassigned to a new post in Berlin, all of which made the deception easier to pull off. As an SS officer I've been in an ideal position to gather intelligence and throw a spanner into the works whenever possible.'

There had always been something uncanny about Sandy's ability to adopt the appearance and mannerisms of another man to the extent that he became a sort of doppelgänger. I knew well from past experience that he was capable of such outrageous deceptions, yet I still had to shake my head at the sheer audacity of this latest gambit.

He gave me an encouraging slap on the shoulder. 'Come on, Dick, we'll stash these bodies in that shed over there. Then we'd best make a move. I'm pretty sure this chap Klingsor is hot on our heels.'

Gabriel and I helped him to drag the bodies out of sight, but as we did so I was painfully aware that Sandy had no inkling as to the identity of the Fury pursuing us – nor of her savage determination to be revenged upon him.

20

THE HUNTING PARTY

———

Sandy exchanged his uniform for a plain brown suit he had secreted in the car and stripped the swastika from the vehicle. Then we set off southwards with him at the wheel. I sat beside him while Gabriel occupied the rear seat.

'If you don't mind my asking, Sandy, where exactly are we headed?'

'I was able to contact an old friend of ours and arrange for him to meet us on the road to Limours,' he explained. 'I'm sure you'll be happy to renew your acquaintance with the Marquis de la Tour du Pin.'

'Turpin!' I exclaimed. It was the nickname Archie had bestowed upon the marquis when he was assigned as the French liaison with our division. I recalled his ferocious Gascon character and his implacable hatred of the Boche. 'He shan't be taking any of this lying down.'

'Far from it,' said Sandy. 'You never heard a man curse his own government so fluently. If we can make our rendezvous with him, he'll see us safely the rest of the way.'

'The chances you have taken with this impersonation, Lord Clanroyden, are almost incalculable,' Gabriel said admiringly. 'I only hope the results have been worth it.'

'Aside from saving our skins, that is,' I added.

'I've managed to pull off one or two tricks,' Sandy answered. 'It's not common knowledge as yet, but the

Germans were poised to smash our troops before we could get them off the beaches at Dunkirk. Fortunately I was able to arrange for Hitler's favourite astrologer to advise him that the planets were not propitious for such an attack and that he should hold off for a couple of days to avoid disaster.'

I shook my head in astonishment. 'Sandy, sometimes I think you're more wizard than man. I'm half surprised you haven't brought the Führer along locked in the boot of your car.'

'If only I could have pulled that off!' Sandy gave a laugh that was like an echo of his exuberant youth. 'Not only is he too well guarded but he has the devil's own luck. There are those in the German high command who retain some good sense and would be glad to be rid of him. There's been talk of how it could be done but time and again they simply funk it.'

Looking closer at his profile, I could see in the lines there, in the slight sinking of his eyes, that this masquerade had been an almost intolerable strain on him and that beneath his bravado he was close to exhaustion.

'I take it from your change of costume that the curtain has come down on your performance as Major Gantz,' said Gabriel.

'Well, it wouldn't do to have some zealous Frenchman take a pot shot at me because he mistook me for the enemy,' said Sandy. 'The fact is that that disguise could only hold up for so long.'

'Time had run out?' I guessed.

Sandy nodded. 'A couple of days ago I ran into one of Gantz's old companions from his days as a junior officer, an annoyingly curious fellow who simply would not be brushed off. He got his suspicions up and started making enquiries about me, so I reckoned I only had a day or two before my cover was blown.'

'So you headed for Paris.'

'I had a coded message from Blenkiron tipping me off that you were on your way here to rescue somebody important. I thought you might need an extra friend watching your back, so I cooked up some bogus orders assigning me here.'

'Your instincts couldn't have been more spot on,' I assured him.

'I heard about a valuable prisoner being busted loose this morning,' Sandy continued, 'so when I caught the message about a pair of men captured fleeing the city, I put two and two together. I gather you've had a run-in with this spy Klingsor who's been giving our side a few headaches.'

My throat went completely dry and I felt sick to my stomach about what I had to tell him.

'Listen, old man, there's something you need to know . . .' I steeled myself to continue. 'Klingsor is a young woman, a rather beautiful and determined young woman named Beata van Diemen. She pretends to be a Dutch exile working against the Reich.'

'A girl, eh?' said Sandy. 'Who would have guessed it?'

'She's not just any woman,' I pressed on, though the words came unwillingly to my lips. 'She's Hilda von Einem's daughter.'

At this I perceived the barest flicker in his eyes and a slight tightening of his jaw.

He said flatly, 'A daughter . . . had no idea.'

I gave him a few moments to absorb this revelation then continued. 'All she knows of her mother is the legend, of her brilliance, beauty and courage.'

'None of that is untrue,' Sandy murmured.

For all that Hilda von Einem was an enemy, for all that she had sought to further inflame a war which had already cost so many lives, there was no denying her magnificence. To Sandy's romantic soul her allure had been almost irresistible. And now she had returned to haunt him once more.

'She knows enough of her mother's death to blame us for it,' I told him, 'you, me and Blenkiron.'

Sandy's voice was barely more than a whisper now. 'I understand how she would feel that way.'

'So, you see,' I went on, 'she's not just out to capture Gabriel for his information, she's consumed by a blazing desire for vengeance . . . especially against you.'

Sandy's fingers gripped the steering wheel tightly, as though to steady himself. At last he rallied and treated me to his boyish smile. 'Not to worry, Dick. She'll have to catch us first.'

To me, who knew him so well, his pain was all too evident. He had the gaunt look of a mystic emerging from a long, harrowing confinement in some desert cave only to find that a further, even more extreme trial awaited him still.

'Once we fall in with Turpin, that will be an end to it,' I assured him. 'Now that her identity is exposed, Beata is useless to her masters. They'll cast her aside and leave her to be consumed by her own bitterness.'

I had little confidence in my words, but Sandy didn't appear to be listening.

'I need to get home to Barbara and little Diana while they can still recognise me.' He was speaking more to himself now than to me. 'And before I forget how to be myself.' He sounded desolate.

'You deserve an end to all this as much as they deserve to have you back for good,' I encouraged him. 'You've done more already than anyone has the right to ask of you.'

Sandy made no reply. He was staring at the road ahead and at some spot beyond that was invisible to me.

When I glanced back at Gabriel I saw in his face that he understood only too well the shadow that had fallen over us. After a spell the young Austrian attempted to lighten the atmosphere.

'Well, Richard, I am eager to meet your friend, the marquis. He sounds like a fine fellow.'

'Oh, he's that, all right,' I agreed. 'He's a keen huntsman and an expert shot. And his wife Adela . . .' I paused, recalling the beautiful daughter of the American financier Julius Victor.

'She belongs to that race that our enemies hate above all others,' said Sandy. 'Turpin's sent her and the children by ship to America where they'll be safe with her father.'

'Good,' said Gabriel solemnly. 'Yet there are far too many who will not escape.'

Sandy said nothing more and we drove on in silence, each absorbed in his own thoughts. We had left the city far behind and were now moving through lush countryside where rose bushes and apple trees blossomed beneath a brilliant blue sky. At any other time I would have been gladdened by the summer landscape, but even the sun did not shine brightly enough to dispel the sense of impending menace.

As this thought crossed my mind there came the dreaded sound of an aircraft approaching.

Sandy immediately shook off his distracted air and became all business. 'We'll slow down a little,' he said, 'to look as innocent as possible. We're just three chaps out for a drive in the country. Dick, see if you can identify him.'

I searched the sky and spotted the plane. It wasn't hard to see the markings as he swooped in low to inspect us.

'It's German,' I reported. 'Messerschmitt.'

'It might be nothing to do with us,' said Gabriel hopefully.

Much as I wanted to believe that, I had the chilling intuition that Beata had picked up our trail and sent this plane on ahead like a hunting dog.

The plane flew past us, following the road ahead. Our eyes were fixed anxiously upon it, hoping it would continue its course and vanish from sight. Instead it made a U-turn and headed back toward us with predatory intent.

'It's this car he's been sent after, for sure,' said Sandy ruefully. 'It looks like trouble is determined to follow us.'

'I've got a feeling there will be a lot more trouble coming down the road after us,' I said. There was no need to say who would be leading the hunt.

'There's forest country further south,' said Sandy.

'That would give us cover if we could only make it that far.'

The plane was drawing closer and there was nowhere to hide. The surrounding countryside was a patchwork of fields and hedgerows with only scattered farm buildings and clusters of trees too scanty to offer cover. The Daimler was like a fox caught in the open. We could only run and take our chances.

'Sandy, it doesn't matter what happens to us,' I said, 'but we can't let Gabriel be captured.'

'I've no idea why they want you so badly, Gabriel,' said Sandy over his shoulder, 'but Dick's word is good enough for me. We'll do our damnedest to get you out of this.'

Even as he spoke the plane descended on us like a bolt of lightning and opened fire. Sandy hit the accelerator and our vehicle leapt forward, thwarting the pilot's aim. Most of the shots peppered the road behind us, but two metallic bangs told me that our rear end had been hit. I twisted about to face our passenger.

'Gabriel, are you all right?' I demanded anxiously.

'Yes, yes, nothing came through,' said Gabriel, running his hands over his arms as if to reassure himself that he was indeed unscathed.

But it was only a temporary reprieve. Behind us the Messerschmitt had come about and was lining up for another attack.

The distance between us closed rapidly. Pressing down on the accelerator, Sandy threw us into a series of sharp swerves, doing his best to evade the next volley. The enemy's engine roared above us and a stream of bullets slashed the Daimler's bonnet to ribbons. The engine was smashed, tyres burst, and we slewed around out of control. The next thing I knew we were pitched headlong into a ditch.

I flung up my arms to shield my face, but even so I crashed painfully against the dashboard with enough force to knock the breath out of me. Gasping for air, I eased myself upright and cast a half-dazed look around me.

The car had come to rest with its battered nose jammed against the bank. The driver's door hung drunkenly open and the seat was empty. Just then Sandy appeared, peering at me over the buckled windscreen.

'Dick, are you hurt?'

He had a cut on his forehead and an ugly bruise on one cheek, but seemed otherwise uninjured.

'Just winded,' I managed to croak. 'How about Gabriel?'

I was relieved when the young Austrian answered for himself, but his report was not encouraging. 'I think I've cracked some ribs,' he murmured. 'And I can't move my left leg.'

'Hang on. We'll soon have you out of here,' Sandy assured him.

He wrenched open the back door and eased Gabriel out.

I clambered out unsteadily, my legs as weak as jelly, my back aching from the crash. When I scanned about me for the plane I saw that it had veered away and was climbing back into the sky, pointed toward Paris. There could only be one reason the pilot had chosen to break off his pursuit.

Sure enough, I looked up the road and saw a pair of speeding saloon cars bearing down on us. 'Company, Sandy!' I warned.

Sandy spotted the danger and quickly took in our surroundings. He pointed to a derelict building close by, its windows broken and the door hanging askew.

'You get Gabriel in there, Dick,' he said, passing the injured Austrian over to me. 'I'll hold them off.'

I put my arm around Gabriel to support him and we made the best speed we could towards the building. Sandy took cover behind our wrecked vehicle and fired a couple of shots at the enemy as they drew closer. The windscreen of the first vehicle smashed, forcing the driver to pull over abruptly; the second vehicle braked behind. Men with rifles and pistols jumped out to return fire and I recognised them as Beata's crew.

The dark angel of vengeance had arrived.

21

THE RETURN OF ODYSSEUS

Shoulder first, I barged through the ramshackle door, dragging Gabriel along with me. He sank to the floor, gripping a nearby window ledge to keep himself upright. Each of us had a pistol taken from the dead SS men, but Gabriel was in no condition to use his. I drew mine and gave Sandy a couple of shots of covering fire. He came dashing towards us on a zigzag path while bullets whizzed overhead. He sprinted the last few yards and threw himself headlong through the door. As I slammed it shut behind him a bullet splintered the wood.

Streaks of light filtered in through the partially boarded windows, outlining dusty shelves and overturned tables. A pair of empty cupboards yawned at us.

'She is here?' asked Gabriel, his face a grimace of pain.

'Yes,' I answered. 'I recognise her men, so she must be with them.'

Sandy and I took a window each on either side of the door, peering through the spaces between the boards.

'I reckon there can't be more than half a dozen of them,' said Sandy, 'and I'm pretty sure I picked one off.'

His estimate looked right to me, though it was hard to be sure. There were a few trees and bushes out there, and the Germans were clinging to cover, only popping up to let off the odd bullet that smacked the outer walls.

'Not the best of shots, are they?' I observed.

Sandy's eyes scanned the dingy interior and fixed on a small door. 'It looks like there's a back way out.'

'Making a run for it looks chancy,' I said, glancing at Gabriel who was trying to haul himself to his feet. I leaned down and helped him up, though he could only stand by leaning against the wall.

'You could get away and find your friend, the marquis,' he said bravely, 'but only if you leave me here. I promise you they will not take me alive.'

Painfully he drew his pistol and squinted through the broken window glass.

'It's a bit soon for that sort of talk,' Sandy told him. 'They don't look like they're in any hurry to rush us.'

He stared out to where one of the Germans was lurking behind a tree, steeling himself to advance further. Sandy took aim and chipped a piece off a branch right by his head. The German ducked back and Sandy gave a grunt of frustration. 'Nearly had him.'

I spotted another man crawling through a patch of long grass and made a hit close enough to send him scrambling back towards his car.

'We're going to have to keep reminding them that we don't want company,' I said.

'They're spreading out,' Sandy warned.

He was right. The Germans were forming a wide arc, making it harder to keep an eye on all of them at once.

'Do you think they're going to make a charge?'

Sandy's brow furrowed. 'More likely they'll try to pin us down while one of them finds a blind side.'

We each took a few more shots, forcing the besiegers to keep their heads down.

'I'm pretty low on ammo,' I said, sliding some shells into my gun.

'Me too,' said Sandy. 'We can't hold them off for much longer.'

'Gentlemen, my friends,' said Gabriel, 'I am sorry you have fallen into this for my sake, but I am honoured to be one of your company.'

He propped himself up on the windowsill, ignoring his injuries and trying to bring his gun to bear. When he fired, unsteady as he was, the recoil almost knocked him over.

'Listen,' said Sandy, 'if you two can keep them busy for a couple of minutes, I'll see if I can sneak out back and outflank them. The element of surprise may be just enough to give us an edge.'

'But if they should spot you,' Gabriel objected.

'You've never watched him stalk a deer,' I told the young Austrian. 'A shadow doesn't move more silently.'

Gabriel was summoning a pained smile when a fusillade hit us. Bullets hacked the door, shattered the remaining panes of window glass, and blasted chunks out of the wooden boards. All of the Germans were firing at once now in a concentrated attack.

Gabriel jerked back reflexively. His injured leg gave way and he tumbled to the floor with a yelp of pain. I was reaching to help him when a bullet smashed through the window and hammered into my right arm. A jolt of agony made me fall to my knees, my gun clattered to the floor, and a red haze covered my eyes.

'Dick, are you all right?' I was aware of Sandy crouching beside me.

'Not so good, I'm afraid,' I groaned, clamping a hand over my wound.

My arm hung limp and useless, a sure sign that the bone had been shattered. As my vision cleared the hail of bullets ceased and a shaft of light broke from the back of the room. The rear door had swung open, and there stood Beata van Diemen. In her hand was a Mauser machine pistol which could cut all three of us down in the blink of an eye.

'Drop your weapons!' she commanded, her voice cutting the air like the crack of a whip.

I had never before seen Sandy turn pale, but now he looked as if he was confronted by a ghost. He saw at once the resemblance I had been so slow to recognise and it froze him on the spot. Then his soldier's instincts took over and he quietly assessed our situation.

Everything in her posture and the steely gleam in her eye told him she would put a bullet in each of us before he could got a shot off. Carefully he set his pistol aside and displayed his empty hands.

Beata, dressed in a plain black jacket, riding breeches and leather boots, looked every inch the huntress I knew her to be. I understood now that the men out front had merely been a distraction, allowing her to creep round to the rear, and the sudden storm of gunfire had been timed to let her enter unnoticed.

She cast a smile of cold satisfaction over her captured quarry. 'There will be no more escapes for you, Graf von Falken. And you, Mr Hannay, you are supposed to be dead.'

She eyed me down the long barrel of her gun, as though deciding whether to finish the job now. Then

Sandy stood up. The moment the pale light touched his face, her expression changed. Her mouth hardened and her eyes flashed like ice.

Sandy took a single step towards her and the air in the room crackled with the shock of their mutual recognition.

'I know who you are,' Beata whispered. 'You are the man my mother called Greenmantle.'

At the uttering of that name Sandy flinched as if he had been struck by a piece of shrapnel.

'I was called that once,' he acknowledged. 'It was a long time ago and very far from here.'

'She offered to lay the world at your feet,' Beata spat, 'to make you an emperor.'

'That is the very offer the devil makes from generation to generation,' said Sandy, almost as if he were channelling the words from somewhere beyond himself. 'A wise man turns away from it.'

'Even a wise man cannot escape his fate, Lord Clanroyden. It is a cruel destiny that has delivered you into my hands.'

'I don't suppose either of us can escape what the past has done to us,' Sandy told her solemnly.

He advanced towards her with slow, deliberate steps, like a pilgrim in fearful awe approaching a sacrificial altar. Gabriel and I lay wounded on the floor, mere witnesses to events that seemed to be moving forward with a relentless inevitability.

Beata's iron composure had been shaken by this unlooked-for encounter, but now she stiffened and levelled her pistol at Sandy. 'Stay back,' she warned imperiously, 'I am quite prepared to kill you right here and now.'

'I don't doubt that at all,' Sandy responded in a voice scarcely louder than a murmur. 'I suppose it would be only just.'

I watched helplessly as the distance between them closed. There was a terrible, elemental quality to their confrontation, as if they met not in some corner of France but in the middle of a sun-blasted desert with an arid, angry wind howling about them. I could hear Sandy speaking to her in German but so quietly I could not make out the words. It was then that she shot him.

Sandy took the bullet in his chest and paused for a split second before falling forward onto Beata. In the same instant I saw a thin blade slip from his sleeve into his right hand. He drove the knife straight into her heart with all the life that was left in him.

Beata's mouth fell open, more in disbelief than in fear. The pair of them crumpled to the floor, locked in their fatal embrace, then slipped apart, each stained with the blood of the other. Beata's dead eyes stared fixedly upward, as if straining for a glimpse of her Valhalla.

I pushed myself up and staggered towards Sandy, falling to one knee beside him. His life's blood was ebbing away but he reached out and took my hand in his. His fingers already felt cold to the touch. He spoke to me in a ghost of his own voice, his eyes wandering about the room as if in search of someone else.

'Dick, tell Barbara I'm coming home at last . . . Tell her that I'll be there . . . to watch over her and Diana . . . always.'

With that final breath his hand went limp and slipped from mine. He was gone, untethered at last from the harbour of this world. My heart sank and I felt shaken to the very bottom of my soul.

Gabriel appeared at my side and crossed himself in the Roman fashion. 'He was a great man.'

'He was that,' I responded in a choked voice.

At that very moment the door was kicked open and the first of Beata's gang stood framed in the doorway with a sub-machine gun in his arms. He took in the scene at a glance and ground his teeth at the sight of his dead mistress. Turning his weapon upon us, he uttered an almost feral growl and began to press the trigger.

I started at the sound of a shot, but it did not come from the German's gun. It was the crack of a high-powered rifle that sent him toppling over, a jet of blood spouting from his shattered skull.

Behind him his companions cried out in alarm and looked frantically about them. They were aware that they were easy targets for whatever unexpected enemy had surprised them. One by one a series of expert shots from a band of unseen marksmen felled them all in a matter of seconds.

Closing Sandy's eyes, I lurched over to the door and saw our rescuers hurrying towards us. At their head, dressed for the hunt and carrying a rifle fitted with a telescopic sight, was my old friend Turpin. With him were three other men with lean tanned faces acquired from years of stalking wild game in the woods and mountains of France.

'By all the saints – Richard!' the marquis exclaimed.

'I should have guessed that when the Boche came you would be here to give them a bloody nose.'

We embraced in the doorway and I winced at the pain in my wounded arm.

'Turpin, I've never been so glad to see a man. Another few seconds would have been too late.'

'We saw the plane from a distance making its attack,' he said, 'and assumed the worst. With all haste we followed the sounds of gunfire and spotted the Boche coming at you.'

Gabriel limped over to join us and I introduced them.

'We shall take you to my lodge and I shall fetch a doctor,' said Turpin. Then he became grave. 'But where is Lord Clanroyden?'

Without a word I led him inside to where Sandy lay in the peace that had eluded him for so long.

'Mon Dieu!' Turpin groaned. 'This is a high price to pay.'

'We can't leave him here,' I said.

'No, we will take him,' Turpin stated firmly. 'We shall see that he returns to his home.'

22

THE FINAL BEGINNING

———

That night we recuperated at Turpin's hunting lodge. He fetched a doctor who patched Gabriel and myself up as well as could be managed for the present. A simple coffin was obtained to hold Sandy's body.

In the morning we set off in a small fleet of cars for Bordeaux. The Germans were too busy consolidating their hold on Paris to press any further south. Moreover, everyone expected the French government to announce an armistice within the next few days that would hand victory over to the invaders without another shot being fired.

Blenkiron's instructions had been to head for the airport at Bordeaux where transportation back to London would be arranged for us. When Turpin dropped us off there, it lifted my spirits considerably to find Archie and the Die-Hards waiting for us. We greeted each other warmly, relieved that we had made it through, if not unscathed.

'You two have taken a few knocks,' said Archie, noting that my arm was in a sling and Gabriel was limping.

'I'm just glad to see you made it out of that farm, Archie,' I said.

'Yes, I managed to get *Antonia* back in the air,' Archie reported proudly, 'but sadly she gave out on me just before Dover. I had to ditch in the sea where some navy tars fished me out and treated me to a shot of rum. It's a damned shame to say goodbye to the old girl, but she did get me home. Almost.'

He gestured towards the runway where a Lockheed Hudson transport plane was waiting for take-off.

'There's my new kite over there. She's a much bigger ship, as you can see. Though I have to confess I'm completely stumped as to what to call her.'

'Did your Aunt Antonia have a sister, perhaps?' I suggested.

'You know, I never thought of that. Let's see . . . Cordelia? No, that won't do. Millicent? Absolutely not! Dash it, something will come to me.'

The Die-Hards had quite an adventure to recount and I was not to hear the entire story until we were in the air. In the meantime Jaikie gave me the gist of it.

The firefight outside Le Pégase had been ferocious, especially when a squad of German troops arrived to take possession of the precious prisoner. Jaikie had made a dash to the roof and shinned down a drainpipe into an alleyway. He dodged his way to where the others were holding out and they took off in their bullet-riddled car.

Fortunately for them, Beata had realised they were merely a diversion and sent all the men at her disposal in pursuit of Gabriel and myself. The damaged Delage gave out after only a few streets and the Die-Hards proceeded on foot.

'I'd caught a bullet in the calf,' said Dougal, 'but Doc patched me up well enough so I could keep up.'

'Knowing that the Germans would be busy occupying key government and strategic positions, Thomas devised a route that got us past them all,' Jaikie explained. 'Dougal and I, during our reconnaissance of the city, had spotted a number of boats tied up along the Seine, and we borrowed one of them to take us beyond the enemy lines.' The normally reticent pastor chipped in with some further explanation. 'They've not had time yet to organise river patrols, so we slipped away with no trouble at all.'

'Once back on land we ran into a French motorised unit making an unhappy retreat westwards,' said Dougal, 'so we threw in with them.'

'And did our best to cheer them up with a few Jacobite songs,' Peter added with a chuckle. 'We Scots know a thing or two about bouncing back from a drubbing.'

We walked across the tarmac towards the plane and Gabriel couldn't help but smile at the Die-Hards as they joked and laughed among themselves.

'I shall never understand the Scots,' he said. 'Their religion is so grim, their country so cold, and yet they are the most romantic of people.'

'If we're going to pull a victory out of this conflagration,' I said, 'we'll need men with that sort of fighting spirit.'

'Richard, one thing above all is very important to me,' Gabriel said earnestly. 'Your prime minister must broadcast a message that will be heard across Europe, a call to resistance, so that all of my friends will know that Roland has arrived safely at the court of Charlemagne.'

'I think I can promise you,' I said, 'that once you've delivered your information about the thirty-one kings, Churchill will have some strong words to say on the subject.'

We all fell silent as we watched Sandy's coffin being loaded aboard the plane.

I was aware of *The Pilgrim's Progress* in my pocket and of Mary's words from many years ago when we strolled together through the St Germain forest. 'Before the pilgrimage can be completed,' she reminded me then, 'the best of the Pilgrims has to die.' For my friend that long journey of hope and hazard was finally over.

For the rest of us it was just beginning anew.

However matters may go in France or with the French Government or with another French Government, we in this island and in the British Empire will never lose our sense of comradeship with the French people. If we are now called upon to endure what they have suffered we shall emulate their courage, and if final victory rewards our toils they shall share the gains, aye. And freedom shall be restored to all. We abate nothing of our just demands – Czechs, Poles, Norwegians, Dutch, Belgians, all who have joined their causes to our own shall be restored.

What General Weygand has called the Battle of France is over ... the Battle of Britain is about to begin. Upon this battle depends the survival of Christian civilisation. Upon it depends our own British life, and the long continuity of our institutions and our Empire. The whole fury and might of the enemy must very soon be turned on us. Hitler knows that he will have to break us in this island or lose the war. If we can stand up to him, all Europe may be freed and the life of the world may move forward into broad, sunlit uplands.

But if we fail, then the whole world, including the United States, including all that we have known and cared for, will sink into the abyss of a new dark age made more sinister, and perhaps more protracted, by the lights of perverted science. Let us therefore brace ourselves to our duties, and so bear ourselves, that if the British Empire and its Commonwealth last for a thousand years, men will still say, This was their finest hour.

WINSTON CHURCHILL'S SPEECH
TO THE HOUSE OF COMMONS, 18 JUNE 1940,
THE DAY AFTER THE FRENCH SURRENDER

AUTHOR'S NOTE

John Buchan wrote five novels featuring Richard Hannay. It has been a privilege to be granted the opportunity to continue his adventures and to introduce him to the Gorbals Die-Hards from Buchan's marvellous *Huntingtower* series. Many thanks to all those without whose assistance Richard Hannay would still be in unhappy retirement.

My wife Debby has been, as ever, my sounding board, chief researcher and most demanding editor. Kirsty Nicol dug up all manner of useful information on everything from train timetables to vintage cars. Elizabeth Wein provided additional aeronautical information. My son Jamie was the one who gave me the nudge needed to get the whole project started. The unfailing enthusiasm of the whole team at Birlinn/Polygon has been a constant source of inspiration. The facilities provided by the University of St Andrews library and the Department of English have greatly helped in the creation of this novel.

Peter's story about the Scotsman and the bucket in chapter eleven is a true story originally told by Gregor Macdonald of the Cameron Highlanders. You can find it on page fifty-five of *St Valery: The Impossible Odds* (ed. Bill Innes, Birlinn, 2011).

For more information on *The Thirty-One Kings* and my other projects, please visit my website at www.harris-authors.com.

R.J.H.